"They really respond well to you," Luke said.

"They're good boys. They have good hearts."

He wanted to tell her that he had a good heart, as well. But so what? Other than that, he didn't have much to offer a woman.

"They've gotten really close to you," he said.

"I know." She sighed. Was that a good sigh or a bad sigh? Luke couldn't tell. "I worry that maybe we've gotten too attached to each other."

"We? You mean you and me?"

"Actually, I was talking about me and the kids," she said, making his chest sink like the toy anchor at the bottom of the hot tub. "Listen, Luke. I really need to tell you something. To explain why—"

"Hold that thought," Luke interrupted, seeing his mom waving at him from the doorway. "The boys are sleeping in the RV with my parents tonight and I need to get them out and dried off before Mom and Dad change their minds."

She held her mouth in a tiny *O* of surprise. And if he wasn't sure where her conversation had been headed, he would've been tempted to kiss the surprise right off her lips. But he really did need to get his kids out of here before Carmen delivered her big thanks-but-no-thanks speech, which would end up breaking more than one Gregson heart.

Dear Reader,

Writing *The Matchmaking Twins* was so much fun for me, especially because I got to channel so much energy into my eight-year-old characters, Aiden and Caden Gregson. I have two boys (not twins) who've caused plenty of mischief and have taught me to cringe every time their school phone number pops up on my caller ID.

But even more compelling for me was to write about Nana Gregson and Abuela. Luke, the hero, had a favorite relative he'd connected with early on during his childhood. And Carmen, the police officer heroine in this story, is not about to be outdone by Luke's bond with his Nana. She invokes quite a few of her own recollections and favorite expressions of her insightful grandmother.

These scenes made me realize that many of us have specific expressions, smells or songs that trigger memories of certain loved ones. Like Luke, I sought solace away from my gaggle of brothers by spending quality time with my aunt Mary Jane. She taught me how to roll hair curlers, how to scour a kitchen sink and how to light her cigarettes for her so she could keep both her nervous hands on the steering wheel of her '74 Lincoln Continental. To this day, the smell of Pond's Cold Cream, Soft Scrub bleach and Kent 100s always make me think of her.

For more information on the other books in the Sugar Falls, Idaho series, visit my website at christyjeffries.com, or chat with me on Twitter, @christyjeffries. You can also find me on Facebook and Instagram. I'd love to hear from you.

Enjoy,

Christy Jeffries

Facebook.com/authorchristyjeffries

Twitter.com/christyjeffries (@ChristyJeffries)

Instagram.com/christy_jeffries

The Matchmaking Twins

Christy Jeffries

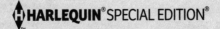

Recycling programs
for this product may
not exist in your area.

ISBN-13: 978-0-373-65971-5

The Matchmaking Twins

Printed in U.S.A.

www.Harlequin.com

Christy Jeffries graduated from the University of California, Irvine, with a degree in criminology, and received her Juris Doctor from California Western School of Law. But drafting court documents and working in law enforcement was merely an apprenticeship for her current career in the dynamic field of mommyhood and romance writing. She lives in Southern California with her patient husband, two energetic sons and one sassy grandmother. Follow her online at christyjeffries.com.

Books by Christy Jeffries

Harlequin Special Edition

Sugar Falls, Idaho

From Dare to Due Date
Waking Up Wed
A Marine for His Mom

To my great-aunt, Mary Jane Templeton.
Thank you for providing me with so much
characterization for this story, and thank you for
providing me with so much love and acceptance as
a child. I miss our shopping trips, our beauty parlor
visits and our lunches out. I'm sure Heaven has a
lot more gold-painted pinecones, Pepsi-Cola and
Grand Ole Opry episodes now that you're there.

Chapter One

Officer Maria Carmen Delgado had once come under heavy fire while guarding some of the most remote military encampments in the world before leaving the Marine Corps to become a cop, patrolling the roughest gang neighborhoods in Las Vegas. But eight-year-old twins Aiden and Caden Gregson of Sugar Falls, Idaho, were certainly going to be the death of her.

"Boys," she said as she unlocked the driver's-side door to her squad car. "I told you that if you were going to ride along with me, you had to promise to stay in the backseat of the Explorer."

"Sorry, Officer Carmen," Aiden said, looking anything but remorseful. "Chief Cooper was calling you on the radio, and we had to tell him that you were ten-seven 'cause you were taking a leak. We couldn't figure out the secret code for the leak part."

When she'd volunteered for the after-school mentorship program at Sugar Falls Elementary, she'd expected to get assigned as a quasi-big-sister to some disadvantaged young girl. She hadn't expected the director to pair her up with a couple of identical little boys with a penchant for mischief and a knack for speaking their overly bright minds.

Normally she only hung out with the Gregson twins when she was off duty. But the officer scheduled to relieve her had come down with the flu and the small-town police department was still new and slightly understaffed, so she'd volunteered to stay late and cover his shift. Since Carmen didn't like letting anyone down, she'd gotten special permission to pick the boys up from school in her patrol vehicle and bring them back to the station. It would only be for an hour, she'd told herself. What trouble could they possibly get into in that amount of time?

She should've known better.

So far, they'd already locked themselves inside a jail holding cell, lost a week's worth of their allowance money by betting the dispatcher she couldn't finish their math homework and got kicked out of the local Gas N' Mart.

And now they'd just told her boss that she'd been taking a leak. Actually, Carmen wished it was just that simple to use the restroom while wearing all her tactical gear along with her police uniform—especially since she went more frequently following her surgery.

Because she couldn't very well take the boys inside the ladies' room with her, she'd told them to stay put inside her cruiser and asked Scooter Deets, one of the older volunteer firefighters who was parked nearby, to keep an eye on the twins. Apparently, ol' Scooter was no better at maintaining control than she was.

Carmen shook her head, thankful the bobby pins securing her coiled bun prevented her hair from being as frazzled as her nerves.

"I knew I never should have let you guys learn our radio codes. You two are in violation of ten-thirty and about to become ten-fifteens," she said, referring to their unauthorized use of police equipment.

"Wait." Caden pulled out the little notepad he'd started carrying in his pocket lately. "What's a ten-fifteen again?"

"It's a prisoner in custody," his twin brother answered before flashing his cheeky smile, minus two recently lost incisors.

"Hey, Officer Carmen, will you teach us Spanish, too?"

"Vámanos, mi liositos," she said before shooing them out of the front and using the handheld radio mic to respond to her boss.

"Sorry about that, Chief," she said after his voice crackled on the other end. "The Gregson twins are officially on administrative suspension for disobeying a direct order to stay put in the *backseat.*"

"Roger that," her boss said. "Tell them that their dad came by the station to pick them up, but since you all were still out, I told Luke that you'd meet him at the Little League fields. You can drop them off there."

Her belly twisted and she resisted the urge to throw the mic out the window. Captain Luke Gregson, the twins' father, was the last person she wanted to see today. Or, really, any day for the matter. But she couldn't say that to Chief Cooper.

"Ten-four," she replied instead, before clicking off. Then she turned to her two mischievous passengers. "Buckle up, kiddos."

"Can we go Code Three with the lights and sirens and everything?" Caden asked as she pulled the vehicle back onto the main highway and headed toward the small park on the other side of town. "Dad's gonna make us do extra laps if we're late to practice."

She should've just taken the boys to the ball fields after school and let them run wild. Maybe if they got more of their energy out, they wouldn't be prone to getting into so much trouble. Not that anyone ever really disciplined the adorable rascals.

And speaking of their lack of discipline, by having to take them directly to baseball practice, she'd be forced to shoot the breeze with their father, the hunky and obviously heartbroken Captain Gregson. It wasn't that there was anything wrong with the handsome and widowed Navy SEAL turned recruiter. Or that Carmen didn't know how to talk to men. It was just that the man had this extremely frustrating habit of treating Carmen like she was one of the guys.

Of course, she couldn't really blame him, or the rest of the males in the small touristy town of Sugar Falls. With her long black hair always pulled into a tight no-nonsense bun and a complete lack of makeup, Carmen was used to working in a male-dominated environment and having to fit in with the good ol' boys.

It was difficult for people to see that beneath the Kevlar vest and the blue polyester unisex uniform, she was still one-hundred-percent female. Keeping one hand on the steering wheel, she rested the other one underneath her sturdy leather duty belt and rubbed along her longest scar. Well, she was *mostly* female.

She took a deep breath, squared her shoulders and tried to focus on the innocent chatter of the eight-year-olds behind her. In her brain, she knew that she was a strong woman and her ability to have children, or lack thereof, should not define her.

But there was always that niggling sense of what she'd lost.

"Hey, Officer Carmen," Caden said, breaking her negative reverie. "Are you gonna be at our game this Saturday? Dad and Coach Alex said I could be lead batter."

Carmen sagged against her seat, wishing she could go to all the twins' games. But no matter how much the two charming troublemakers were growing on her, she'd rather relive her emergency surgery than be faced with spending more time near their father, Captain Dimples.

Luke had returned to town only a month after she'd taken the position with the Sugar Falls Police Department. When she'd been in the Marine Corps, she'd heard about his elite Special Ops team who'd carried out some of the deadliest missions in Afghanistan. Of course, she hadn't thought that one of its members would eventually end up living in the same small city. Or that said member would have such adorable kids, who needed more supervision than the single dad could provide.

She especially didn't know that he'd be so damn good-looking.

"I'm not sure about this weekend," Carmen said. "We'll see what my schedule looks like."

"Aw, c'mon, Officer Carmen," Aiden chimed in. "Ever since Aunt Kylie had her babies, we're the only kids on the team who don't have someone in the stands cheering for us."

Her chest grew heavy with guilt and she tugged on her weighted vest as if she could physically relieve the pressure. Here she'd been feeling sorry for herself and the fact that she'd never have a family of her own, yet these poor young children had to grow up without a mom. As much as she'd bonded with the two wild and wonderful boys, was she doing them all a disservice by allowing herself to get too close to them when what they really needed was a mother figure?

She was usually much more empathetic than this, which was why she'd been a good MP and an even better cop in Vegas. It was why she'd made the big move to a small town like Sugar Falls in the first place. She needed to find herself again.

And she needed to get her emotions in check.

She pulled into the dirt lot behind the bleachers and was saved from making any additional commitments by the sudden appearance of the tall, muscular, blond male walking toward them and waving.

Her stomach grew uncomfortable and she almost undid her seat belt, thinking the baton attached to her duty belt had shifted and was digging into her flesh. But she knew the feeling well enough to realize it wasn't from anything she was wearing. She got that same tightening of her insides every time she saw Captain Luke Gregson.

"Hey, monkeys," he said to his children as he leaned into the open driver's-side window. "Did you guys catch any crooks today?" His face was close enough that she could see where he'd cut himself shaving this morning. And she could smell the lemon and oak moss scent of his aftershave.

Button it up, Delgado, she told herself.

"Well, we almost stopped a robbery at the Gas N' Mart," one of the kids said from the backseat. But Carmen was so focused on not attaching her nose to the tanned and fragrant skin on Luke's neck that she couldn't tell which of the boys was talking. "We were getting our slushies and a man walked in with his hat pulled down past his eyebrows and he was reaching into his back pocket, like he was gonna pull out a gun."

Luke raised one brow, clearly aware of his children's fondness for exaggeration. Carmen should interject here, but she was too busy commanding her tummy to relax to get any words out.

"So, me and Caden made a run for him, 'cause we were gonna karate chop him up before he could start shooting down the place."

"Oh, crap," Luke muttered, and she finally got her hormones under control so she could explain.

"Don't worry." She put her hand up as though she could physically stop his thoughts. Then she returned it to the wheel when she realized how close it was to touching his face. "It was only Scooter Deets, and he was reaching for his wallet, not a gun."

"Yeah, but we didn't recognize him 'cause he wasn't wearing his normal Boise State cap. His new goat chewed a hole clean through it, and now he has to wear a diff'rent one until he goes into the big city next month."

The big city was Boise. It was only an hour's drive

down the mountain, but it was probably a yearly excursion for a local like Scooter.

"So nobody actually got hurt?" Luke asked. Was it her imagination or was his sudden release of air a little too warm and minty? "There wasn't any damage?"

"Well, Scooter didn't really get hurt 'cause we landed on all those chips when we jumped at him. But Mrs. Marconi told Officer Carmen that someone was gonna hafta pay for a new display stand since hers is all bent up now."

Luke drew his fingers through his short military-cut hair. Carmen had seen the exasperated mannerism several times just this past month and knew the poor dad was once again frustrated at his children's antics. "Okay, boys. Hop out and go warm up for practice. I already put your gear in the dugout."

"Do we hafta do extra laps?" Aiden wanted to know as they exited her car.

"You will if you don't mind your manners and thank Officer Delgado for putting up with you two this afternoon."

"Thanks, Officer Carmen," Aiden said. Ever since she'd taken the job with the police department, the twins were the only people in town who called her by her first name. Well, actually her middle name, since Maria Carmen was a mouthful even to her.

"Yeah, thanks," Caden added. "We'll see you next Tuesday again. And maybe Saturday for the game, remember?"

After this afternoon, she was looking forward to a little peace and quiet. But would it really be almost a whole week before she'd get to see them again?

"I'll see you next Tuesday, but I don't know about

Saturday, yet." Unfortunately, her last sentence wasn't even heard by the two boys who were now running toward their teammates.

"So, do I really have to pay for a new chip display at the Gas N' Mart?" Luke asked.

Uh-oh. He was still there. And her little towheaded buffers had made a beeline for the field. She shifted her hips to the right, but because of her holster knocking into the seat belt buckle, she couldn't scoot any farther away from him.

"It really didn't look too busted to me," she said, thankful she was wearing her mirrored aviator sunglasses. Hopefully Luke couldn't tell that she was barely able to make eye contact with him. "I set it back up and the boys put all the bags that didn't burst open back on the shelves. I was going to have them clean up the broken chips, but I think Elaine Marconi just wanted us to get out of there at that point. She was annoyed, but she has kids of her own so she didn't seem too put out. I'll have the chief let you know if she files a claim for damages."

There. She'd directed any future conversation through her boss, who also happened to be Luke's friend. While she loved spending time with his funny and impulsive children, being around the man himself caused the butterflies fluttering around in her stomach to migrate straight to her brain.

"Those boys are going to be the death of me," he said, voicing aloud the exact thought she'd had forty minutes ago. His forearms now rested on her windowsill, as though he wasn't planning to shove off anytime soon.

"Anyway, I'm sorry we're late. It was my fault," she

said quickly, hoping he'd take the hint that she was in a hurry to finish the conversation.

"Don't worry about it. Listen, I really appreciate you spending time with them after school. I'm sure you have much more important things to do around town than play big sister to a couple of little monkeys." The way he smiled showed his dimples to advantage and indicated that he used the nickname for his kids out of affection.

But she wasn't particularly fond of the way he classified her into his sons' peer age range, as if she wasn't just a few years younger than Luke, himself. At least he'd said *sister*, though, and not *brother*. That was something, right?

As much as she wanted to get far, far away from his sexy grin, politeness dictated she respond. "Actually," she said, "you may find this hard to believe, but the Sugar Falls PD doesn't see too much action on the weekdays. Foiling a nonrobbery at the Gas N' Mart has been the most exciting thing to happen on one of my shifts since last January when those tourists didn't check out of the Snow Creek Lodge by eleven o'clock."

She clamped her lips tightly together after she spoke. Why did she do that? Why did she always downplay the importance of her job—the value of her abilities? Shrinks would probably say it was some type of residual defense mechanism from growing up in her oversize machismo family or trying not to stand out in a male-dominated profession.

"Still, I know they're in good hands with you." Did the man ever stop smiling? "Coop said you outwrestled half his force in defensive tactics training last week."

"That's not saying much considering we only have

four other officers on staff." There she went again. She should be proud that she was an expert in martial arts. But she didn't want Luke to think of her as some juiced-up, studly gladiator. She wanted him to see her as…

Stop. It was this kind of foolish thinking that would seriously undermine all the work she'd put into getting her mind right and her head back in the game since she'd broken up with Mark and moved here. Man, she needed to get away from Luke and her AWOL thoughts.

Thinking quickly, she reached beneath the dashboard and double clicked on the mic of her bandwidth radio, causing the volunteer dispatcher to respond. Carmen clicked on the mic again, then leaned down toward the radio as though she was listening to something Luke couldn't hear.

The resulting static probably wouldn't fool a former SEAL, but she went through the pretense of answering a phony call out. "Ten-four. I'm en route."

She looked back at him as she put the vehicle in gear. "Gotta run," she said, barely waiting for him to move his arms off the window before tearing out of the dirt lot.

That was the worst fake radio call out Luke had ever seen. And he should know. He'd trained as a communications specialist before going through Basic Underwater Demolition/SEAL training.

He watched Officer Delgado drive off, gravel crunching and dust flying. Why had she been in such a hurry to get away from him? Was he giving off that lonely "I need to talk to someone who understands kids" vibe again? He rubbed his forehead, then dragged his fingers through his hair before shoving his hands in his jeans pockets.

His twin brother, Drew, said it was obvious whenever Luke was missing the guys from his unit—or worse, when he'd been in the cabin all weekend with his squirrelly sons and he needed adult conversation—because it was the only time Luke uttered more than a few sentences.

But moving to Sugar Falls to become a full-time dad, changing assignments from team leader of an elite Special Forces unit to pushing paper at the naval recruiting office outside of Boise…well, it was all proving to be more challenging than he'd anticipated.

Luke poked his athletic shoe at some tiny rocks that had been kicked up from Carmen's patrol car as she'd blasted out of the lot. The action was instinctive, as though his feet needed the physical reminder that he was actually standing on solid ground.

He thought back to the night before Samantha's accident several years ago. Luke had been in a training exercise where the team was being hoisted from the ocean and into a hovering Osprey helicopter. It was dark and the water was choppy, with waves crashing over his head. When it had been his turn, part of his safety harness ripped and he'd had to hold on to the cable with his bare hands to keep from dropping. He'd dangled like that, with the chopper blades stirring up more wind force than the actual storm, for at least a minute before being pulled up to safety.

Ever since his wife had died, he hadn't been able to shake that feeling of being suspended in the air, swinging above a raging dark sea and holding on as if his life depended on it.

"Hey, Dad," Aiden yelled from the outfield. "Are ya comin' or what?"

He waved at the boy and started to jog toward the dugout. He needed a good run tonight. Something that would clear his thoughts or at least make his mind too tired to think.

"How's Officer Delgado today?" Alex Russell, the team coach, asked Luke when he finally made it back to the dugout. He liked Alex, whose family owned the local sporting goods store, but he didn't like the sly half smile the man was now wearing.

"What's that supposed to mean?" Even Luke heard the unfamiliar agitation in his voice.

"I've just noticed that she's been dropping the boys off at practice a few weeks in a row."

"Yeah, that mentorship program at the school finally found someone who was willing to take them on. Once a week, I have to stay at the recruiting office later and can't pick the boys up, so I think Delgado must've taken pity on them—the people who work at the after-school program, that is."

"Some kids have all the luck."

His kids? Lucky? No way. They'd already lost their mom before they could really remember her and they'd been bounced around with various relatives while Luke had played Captain Save-the-World. Now it was taking a whole ski resort village to raise the lovable little hellions. "What do you mean?"

"Not only do they get to hang out with a cop, which would be any boy's dream, but they get to ride around with the hottest one on the force."

"Officer Delgado?" Okay, so Luke was faking the surprise in his voice. The woman was naturally beautiful with those classic high cheekbones and full lips, but he'd quickly gotten the impression from the woman herself, as well as most of the other men in town, that she definitely was not on the market—not that *he* was, either. So then why was Alex bringing up her hotness?

"C'mon. Like you haven't noticed the way she fills out that uniform."

Sure he had, and he wanted to take the aluminum bat leaning against the fence and swing it at the head coach for even suggesting that he'd noticed, too.

Whoa. *Shake it off, Gregson.* What was up with the irrational jealousy?

"I try not to," Luke said, his jaw locking around each word. And that was true. He felt guilty sometimes just for looking at her.

"Hell, we all *try* not to, Luke. She obviously isn't the type to flaunt anything and probably wouldn't appreciate it if we were noticing. She's all business, that one." Alex picked up a glove and patted his shoulder before walking out of the dugout. "Let's get started, boys!"

Maybe Luke wasn't the only guy in town who Officer Delgado wasn't warming up to. He should be somewhat relieved that it wasn't just him. Still, the woman turned into a block of ice whenever he spoke to her, and he didn't know what to make of that. Luke wasn't usually so chatty, but he'd tried to talk to her about things they could possibly have in common—like the military or martial arts. Once, he even asked her what she bench-pressed because, clearly, the shapely woman worked out. Yet, unless they were talking about the twins, she shut down completely every time.

She'd made it plain that she was indifferent to him, but for some damn reason, anytime he was within a few feet of her, he couldn't get his mouth to stop yapping.

Not that he was actually interested in Carmen like that. Or in any woman, for that matter. When he'd been active on the team and going to bars with his single buddies, he'd had no problem charming the ladies. But those days were over soon after he'd met Samantha.

After his wife died, it had taken him a while to get his head back on straight, and he wasn't entirely convinced he'd succeeded yet. He used to think that volunteering for the most dangerous missions and staring his fears in the face would make him feel more in control. Then, after a near-death experience last summer, he realized he couldn't be so selfish as to put Aiden and Caden at risk of becoming total orphans. So he'd settled down and aimed for the safety net of Sugar Falls.

Now all his charm was exclusively used for smoothing over the trouble his children unintentionally caused. So far, neither his charm nor his commitment to his children had diminished that dangling, out-of-control feeling he still got. To make matters worse, when Carmen Delgado was around, his safety net seemed further away than ever—and he wasn't sure he could survive another free-fall.

Chapter Two

Carmen had just finished lunch at the Cowgirl Up Café on Snowflake Boulevard and was walking back to the station to do some paperwork before her shift was over when a very pregnant Mia McCormick waved her over from across the street.

"Hey, Officer Delgado, you're just the person I wanted to talk to," Mia said as she held open the door to the Sugar Falls Cookie Company to allow Kylie Gregson, the twins' aunt, to maneuver her double stroller inside. "Do you have a second?"

"Sure." Carmen followed the women into the little shop that brought so much business to Sugar Falls. She inhaled the scent of vanilla and looked around at the cute displays to see what the flavor of the month was. She'd always been a sucker for fresh baked goods, and even though the turkey sandwich and potato salad she'd finished a few minutes ago threatened to pop open the button on her uniform pants, she might order a couple of cookies and save them for later.

She tried to look anywhere but at the other customers who cooed and made googly eyes at the twin baby girls, talking to Kylie and Mia about feedings and diapers and all the things Carmen would never get to experience.

Carmen had never felt like such an outsider, which was saying something considering she'd been the only female in her MP unit and had had to hoof it clear across the base to take a shower in the women's head while all of her coworkers got to use the communal locker room.

At least as a Marine and a cop, she had the job in common with her male counterparts. But there was absolutely nothing she could say at that second that would make her fit in with this duo of mommies. And she never would.

When the customers finally left, Mia said, "I'm so behind schedule. I should've taken Maxine up on her offer to deliver the cookies to the old Remington Theater for tonight's dance recital."

Maxine owned the Sugar Falls Cookie Company and was married to Carmen's boss. Since Carmen knew Chief Cooper was off duty this afternoon to accompany his wife to an obstetrician appointment, she doubted the pregnant dance teacher would get much help running errands. Maybe that's what Mia wanted to talk to her about. But before Carmen could remind the woman she was on duty, the other mom spoke up.

"Thank goodness you got the city council to okay you using the old theater for performances," Kylie said to Mia as she rocked her stroller back and forth. She directed her next comment at Carmen. "Sometimes I worry about my girls growing up in a small city with a limited access to culture, so having a legitimate venue for school plays and band concerts is a total win. Last year, when the community center got double booked, we had to watch the fifth grade's talent show while the bingo club was shouting out B-39 and O-14 the whole time."

Carmen smiled politely as the women laughed. She hadn't been in Sugar Falls very long, so she didn't share the same memories, but she appreciated these ladies including her in the conversation and not making her feel so out of the loop. Although she was still waiting for them to clue her in on why they wanted to talk to her.

"You're from Vegas originally, right?" Kylie asked before reaching into the stroller and unstrapping the infant who'd started fussing. Carmen nodded but averted her eyes quickly for fear that if she watched the tender maternal moment too long, she wouldn't be able to look away. In which case, they'd probably see the hunger and the desperation in her eyes. She planned to avoid that scenario. Sympathy was never easy for her to handle.

"Hey, I thought I saw my nieces being wheeled in here," a masculine voice said from the doorway. Carmen didn't have to turn around to recognize the speaker. Her stomach's telltale reaction to his voice already alerted her.

She told herself it was due to the big lunch she'd just consumed, not his unexpected arrival. Just like it was the sudden crisp spring air rushing in from the open door that caused the shiver to race from inside her starched collar all the way down her spine—not Luke Gregson, himself.

Maybe if she repeated that lame excuse eight more times, she might actually believe it.

The tall man was dressed in his blue battle dress uniform, looking like he'd spent all morning modeling in a photo shoot for some Navy recruitment poster. She would think that seeing him in his military uniform would trick her mind into believing that he was just like every other guy she'd worked with over the past ten years.

But judging from the second shiver making its way down her back, it wasn't her mind doing the thinking.

A sudden wail jerked Carmen's attention from the muscular male legs tucked into shiny black boots and toward the small bundle of pink still strapped in the stroller.

"Oh, no." The pitch in Luke's normally deep voice raised a few octaves as he reached for his other niece, talking to her. "Did your mean ol' mama pick up your sister and leave you behind all alone in this big contraption?"

"Luke Gregson." Kylie stood up even taller than her five-foot-ten height as she faced her brother-in-law. "If you call me or my fashionable stroller 'old' one more time, I will drive straight to the school and tell your sons that you promised to take them and five of their best friends camping this weekend."

"Aw, come on, Kylie." Luke's voice sounded just like his sons last week when Carmen had told them they had to practice their spelling words before she took them to Noodie's Ice Cream Shoppe. "That's not cool. It's supposed to rain this weekend, and you know what happened last time I let them invite a friend— one friend—for a sleepover at the cabin. I still have mustard and toilet paper stuck to the living room ceiling."

Carmen laughed. It didn't take much to imagine how Aiden and Caden had managed that.

"Hey, Officer Delgado." Luke finally turned his warm gaze to her. Seeing him holding that precious baby made her stomach drop to her knees, which was the only explanation for why her legs felt so unsteady. "I didn't expect to see you in here chitchatting the afternoon away with these two."

Didn't he? If he saw his sister-in-law and nieces enter the cookie shop, then he had to have seen Carmen come in right behind them. More than likely, he was probably surprised to see her socializing with other women. Not that she wasn't a little surprised herself.

"First, you call me old and now you suggest we're all just wasting our time talking about important town business?" Kylie tried to sound stern. "Give me my daughter, Luke. She can't wait to surprise her cousins at school with the news of their fun-filled weekend."

Luke maneuvered himself and the pink bundle nestled on his shoulder behind Carmen, as though she were the barrier that would protect him from his brother's wife, who was clearly only feigning her annoyance. His dimpled smile struck again.

"Now, now, Kylie. You couldn't ever get mad at me. That's just the hormones talking." When his sister-in-law chuckled, Luke finally moved back into the line of fire. "I remember when Samantha had just given birth to the boys and she called my commanding officer in the middle of the night, reading him the riot act because I was still on deployment and she was out of baby wipes and didn't have any clothes not covered in spit-up that she could wear to the store."

"Your wife was a saint for putting up with you gone on all that secret assignment mumbo jumbo. I couldn't even imagine what I'd do if Drew got deployed before the girls go off to graduate school."

Luke rocked back on his heels but didn't say a word. He didn't have to. The sadness in his blue eyes and the steeliness of his jaw did the talking for him.

"Oh, my gosh, Luke." Kylie must've seen the same hurt expression cross his face because she tenderly stroked his arm. "I am so sorry. I didn't mean it like that."

"It's okay, Kylie. I know what you meant. And you're right. Samantha *did* put up with a lot."

If Carmen had felt mildly awkward before, she was downright uncomfortable at being a witness to his heartache. What was she doing here, anyway? Should she even be listening to them reminisce about his deceased wife, a woman who obviously deserved the pedestal they'd all placed her on?

"So, Mia," Carmen said, trying to verbally tiptoe her way out of the emotional land mine. "What was it you wanted to talk to me about?"

"Oh, that's right. Sorry, I have pregnancy brain and can barely hold on to a passing thought."

Carmen, knowing she would never be able to personally relate to such a symptom, had no response to that statement. Instead, she forced a smile toward the sweet woman.

"You know how we do group exercise classes at the dance studio?" Mia asked but didn't wait for a response. "Well, I normally teach a yoga class on Monday mornings, but with the baby due soon, I'm trying to find some substitute instructors while I'm on leave."

"But I've never taught yoga."

"Delgado's a Marine," Luke said, apparently listening in on their conversation. Kylie must've decided to distract him from his grief because now he was holding both babies, one nestled against each thick bicep. *Whoa.*

"She's a devil dog," he continued. "They don't do sissy yoga. Right, Delgado?"

She cringed slightly at the Marine nickname and his inaccurate assessment of her.

"Easy there, skipper," Carmen said, throwing a naval moniker right back at him. His use of her last name was all the proof she needed that she'd been placed in the Friendzone. It was also a good reminder that she shouldn't be lusting over him. "You just got out of trouble with Kylie and now you're trying to pick a fight with Mia, as well? I think you're underestimating your battle odds."

Mia's hand shot between them like a white flag of surrender. "That's not what I meant. I was actually moving yoga to a different day, which leaves Mondays open. So, I was thinking that maybe you could lead some sort of kickboxing type class or teach self-defense. You know, that type of thing?"

"Oh," Carmen said, at a loss for words. She hadn't been expecting the request. She was flattered that the dance instructor thought her capable of teaching, and a little pleased that the small community was beginning to welcome her into their folds. But still. Would other ladies in town even be interested in such a class?

"Give it some thought." Mia, probably sensing her hesitation, quickly added, "I have the recital tonight, and then the girls and I normally get together on Thursdays for dinner. Why don't you meet with us tomorrow and we can discuss things more?"

"And by discuss things," Kylie added, "she means maybe we can help her talk you into it."

"Uh-oh, Delgado." Luke smiled showing a single dimple. "These women are trying to get you to come over to the dark side with them. I'm sure you'd rather hang out with us tomorrow at poker night."

And there she had it. She knew he was part of the group of men who got together with Chief Cooper once a week to play cards. Which meant Luke Gregson definitely thought of her as one of the guys.

It should feel good that both groups wanted her presence at their Thursday night rituals. But there was still the underlying reminder that the man she couldn't stop thinking about didn't reciprocate her feelings—and probably never would, considering the loving way he spoke of his late wife. It was enough to dash all hope of her ever finding a man who would accept a damaged woman.

In the past ten years, Carmen had had her share of poker nights and locker-room jokes and testosterone-fueled bragging. A night out with the girls actually sounded like a nice change of pace.

So she looked at the two women and, for the first

time, stepped over the invisible line she believed had been drawn in the sand. "What time should I be there, ladies?"

Could Officer Delgado try any harder to avoid him?

As Luke stood outside the bakery, he had to wonder what he'd done to annoy the beautiful cop. Sure, he enjoyed his sassy sister-in-law and her group of friends. But Carmen didn't seem like the type of woman to hang out with a bunch of former cheerleaders turned moms.

She had way more in common with him, and he'd simply been trying to point that out. Okay, so maybe he sounded like an arrogant tool with all that ooh rah Marine business. He wasn't trying to be a chauvinist or imply that she wasn't capable of teaching yoga. From what he'd seen of her with the twins, and from what he'd heard of her reputation with the MPs, she was one tough cookie.

So then why did she always act like he was a melted chocolate chip stuck to the bottom of her black utility boot?

He would've asked Kylie if he'd done anything to offend Carmen, but she'd sat down to nurse one of the girls and Luke had gotten the heck out of Dodge. Not that he was uncomfortable with seeing a woman breast-feed. At least, he doubted he would be. He'd been on a classified mission when his own boys were born, and by the time he'd come home, Samantha had decided that formula was much easier for her. And who was he to object? He couldn't be there all the time and he still felt immeasurable guilt that his wife had had to do everything on her own.

Not that she'd totally been on her own, he'd found out after the fact. Still, it had been a hell of a lot more than he'd done.

When Aiden and Caden were babies and toddlers, Luke was usually only home for a couple of months at a time. He and his late wife didn't necessarily share the same parenting philosophy, but they also didn't share the same workload when it came to the kids, so he took a backseat to her softer approach. Then, after her accident, he'd stayed home long enough to help the boys get through the initial grief before his parents convinced him they could help out. Luke had told himself that the three-year-olds needed a mother figure more than they needed him—after all, it was Samantha who had done most of the work so far.

So when Aiden and Caden were staying with different family members and babysitters and he was still out of the country half the time, the boys lost even more structure.

His cell phone rang, and when he saw the number for the elementary school on the display screen, Luke wished for the thousandth time that he'd been more on top of their discipline. He loved his children more than anything, but man, were they magnets for trouble.

"Captain Gregson, here," he answered.

"Hello, Captain. This is Mrs. Dunn, the nurse over here at Sugar Falls Elementary."

Thank God, it was the nurse this time, and not the principal. Wow, *that* was a really bad thought. "Are my sons okay?" he asked.

"Yes, everyone is fine. Now. Caden had a little incident on the tetherball court and Aiden tried to help him get untangled and, well, the rope got caught. Anyway, I think it's just a bad sprain, but you should probably get some X-rays just in case."

"Which one?"

"The left one."

"I mean, which of my children got injured."

"Aiden has the actual sprain, but from the way Caden is carrying on, you'd think he was the one hurt."

It was a twin thing. Luke and Drew had experienced the similar phenomenon growing up. And even as adults.

"I'm coming right now. Is his arm in a sling?"

"Uh, no. Why would it be?"

Luke only had basic medic training to assist in emergencies until a corpsmen got to the scene, but it would seem to him like the nurse would at least want to take pressure off the injured body part. "I just thought that maybe it would help stabilize his arm."

"Oh, sorry, Captain Gregson. I should've been clearer. The sprain is to Aiden's ankle."

"How in the world did he sprain his ankle with a tetherball rope?"

"That's a great question, Captain. And as soon as he gets his brother to relax, maybe Aiden can tell us. I had to snatch some pudding cups out of the school cafeteria to help in the calming-down process."

"I'll be right there."

Luke disconnected the call, got into his nana's brown Oldsmobile and drove less than a mile from downtown to the school. He'd grown up in Boise, but his parents owned a cabin here and he had spent most of his summers in Sugar Falls before joining the Navy.

While the town setting was familiar, he was still getting used to the slower pace of life.

He would've preferred to drive around in the yellow Jeep his family kept at the cabin, but when his brother, Drew, had stepped in to care for the boys last summer during Luke's last deployment, his overly cautious and analytical brother had insisted that the thirty-year-old sedan was safer for shuttling children than the fun and masculine four-by-four.

At least the Oldsmobile was in good shape. Before she'd passed away ten years ago, his grandmother had only driven the thing three times a week—to the grocery store, to the beauty shop and to the casino out on the reservation—so it had low mileage and only some minor dings in the right front fender. Nana never could make the tight turn into her carport at the mobile home park.

He kept meaning to buy a more functional and fuel-efficient car, especially since he was making the hour-long commute into Boise four times a week. But, contrary to what Drew and their sister, Hannah, thought, he'd always been Nana's favorite grandkid and he missed the old gal.

Growing up, Luke had been the naughty twin— the proverbial pastor's son who drove his mother to distraction. Nana would come pick him up to give his mom a break, calling him her wild child and having him light her menthol cigarettes for her so she could keep both hands on the steering wheel.

He took a deep breath, still able to smell the Benson & Hedges along with the lingering scent of her Shalimar perfume. His parents were fair and loved him, but Nana had been his island—his place to escape. Driving this brown beast made him feel closer to her.

When he pulled into the school lot, he gunned the eight-cylinder engine, just like she used to do, before pulling into a parking spot. He also overestimated his turn radius and the right bumper knocked into the custom sign that read Principal Parking Only.

Yep, just like Nana.

He walked inside and waved at the school secretary, who, after the third week of school, had programmed Luke's cell number into her phone's speed dial.

He let out a little sigh of relief when he turned left to go to the nurse's office instead of heading straight down the hall toward the principal's. He'd spent plenty of time sitting outside doors just like that one when he was growing up. And, since history seemed to be repeating itself, his children had a tendency to do the same.

Karma was definitely on the upswing with his genetics. Luke's parents often referred to it as God's sense of humor.

When he entered the room, he saw Aiden, the injured twin, sitting behind Mrs. Dunn's desk and showing her how to play a computer game. Caden, the uninjured one, was propped on the cot and eating a chocolate pudding cup. His left foot was elevated on several pillows with an ice pack balanced precariously on top.

Even Luke's brother, Drew, a well-respected Navy psychologist, couldn't explain twin telepathy. But both he and Luke had experienced it firsthand and he didn't doubt for a second that Caden could legitimately feel his brother's pain.

Although, from the way Aiden was swinging around in the nurse's chair and yelling commands at the woman on how to fight the Creepers on her computer, it seemed nobody was really the worse for wear.

"Dad? Oh, good. You're finally here," Caden said as he sat up and reached for his backpack. "We need to get Aiden to the hospital for some X-rays. Let me see your phone."

Luke patted his pocket, ensuring his cell was far out of reach from his dramatic and impulsive son. "Who were you planning to call?"

"Officer Carmen. I'm gonna tell her we need a police escort with lights and sirens and the works."

Luke raised his blond eyebrow at Aiden, who had just high-fived Mrs. Dunn for reaching the next level on his favorite game. "I think your brother will be fine on the way there. We can forgo the Code Three routine."

Besides, he was pretty sure Carmen was off duty by now. Wait. How had he known that? Had she mentioned her schedule to him when he'd seen her at the cookie shop earlier?

Considering she hadn't said more than two words to him, he doubted it. So why did he know what her shift was? Because today was Wednesday. And she always worked the afternoon shift on Sundays and Mondays, then the morning shifts on Tuesdays and Wednesdays.

He tapped his toe against the linoleum. Yep, the ground was still solid. So then maybe he could stomp out some of this useless information he was carrying around about a woman who would just as soon do fifty pull-ups than say hello to him.

Of course he would know her schedule because Tuesdays were the days she always picked up the boys after school, right after putting in a ten-hour day. He had to give the woman credit for that. She was an absolute sweetheart with the twins and had the patience of Job. Aiden and Caden couldn't stop talking about her or singing her praises, which was probably why she kept popping up in Luke's head so often—just like his renewed knowledge of *Star Wars* sequels, now that he'd shown the DVDs to the boys.

"Sorry to have to bother you at work, Captain," Mrs. Dunn, the fiftysomething-year-old former Ski Potato Queen, said. He knew she had been on the homecoming court and had earned her crown at the annual ski festival the same decade his grandmother had bought her Oldsmobile because the woman kept the framed pictures and newspaper articles displayed on a shelf right above the bandages and antiseptic wipes.

"Actually, we had a presentation at one of the high schools this morning so I was off early today."

"Being a recruiter must be so exciting. Helping all those young people find their careers." When the nurse smiled at him, he noticed some of her coral lipstick had smeared onto her front two teeth, but he didn't have the heart to point it out to the former beauty queen. When it came to those holding any sort of authority position over his children, he found it best to keep them locked in as allies.

"That's sweet of you to say. It really makes me appreciate all you school employees do to help shape the minds of our next generation." Which was true. Luke loved his own boys, but he didn't think he could deal with so many students and their high-energy personalities on a daily basis. He gave the woman his best get-out-of-trouble smile.

Her mascara-clumped eyelashes fluttered as best they could and he knew he'd hit his mark. She smiled back and said, "I bet the high schoolers just adore having a hotshot hero like you come speak to them."

In Luke's mind, being a SEAL wasn't such a big deal. He had just been doing what he loved. Still, maybe he could ask Nurse Dunn to share her flattering insight with Officer Delgado. Not that he cared what the female cop thought of him.

"Dad?" Aiden tapped him with a one of the crutches he must have borrowed from the school nurse. "You ready?"

"Oh. Um, yeah." After hearing the nurse explain to Caden that she only had one set of crutches, Luke carried Aiden's backpack and watched as his injured eight-year-old hobbled in front of him on one foot. His other son trailed behind with only a slight limp.

Anytime he had a slow day at the recruiting office and thought he missed the excitement of Spec Ops, all he had to do was drive home to his children. No amount of skilled warfare training could have prepared him for the adventure that was fatherhood.

Of course, it was times like these when he wished he'd pursued sniper school. Maybe then he'd be better equipped to work without a teammate. Without a partner. Sure, he had his family for backup, but sometimes he felt so alone.

The kids climbed into the back of Nana's Oldsmobile and then immediately turned the crutches into dueling lightsabers.

It was going to be a very long night.

Chapter Three

"Hey, Officer Carmen, you wanna sign my cast?" Luke heard Aiden say to the long-legged curly-haired brunette wearing tight jeans and high-heeled boots. Caden rushed inside Patrelli's Italian Restaurant to join his brother before Luke could stop them.

Crap. It was bad enough that the boys talked about their cop friend all the time, but now they were so eager to see her, they were mistaking her for random ladies in town. Albeit, a very curvaceous and sexy random lady. Luke let go of the heavy oak door and hurried over to the hostess stand to prevent his son from creating an embarrassing situation.

"Monkey, that's not... Oh." Luke stopped when the woman turned around.

Wow. He'd never seen Carmen wear anything besides her police uniform—something that clearly hadn't been tailored with such a womanly form in mind—or track pants and long-sleeved T-shirts when he'd caught glimpses of her out running.

"It's just a stupid ACE bandage," he heard Caden say, yet the pending argument barely registered in Luke's ears.

Double wow. The woman really had some nice legs.

"Yeah, but I'm pretending it's a cast," Aiden said. "Casts are cooler and way tougher."

"I would love to sign your pretend cast." Carmen reached for a pen off the hostess stand and bent down to write.

Luke had once been skilled at utilizing all five of his senses in any given situation, but try as he might, his eyes were the only thing functioning at that moment. And they were shamelessly staring at Carmen's, ah, assets. She had on some type of loose, flowing, purple top, and from this angle, he could see down to where the rounded curves of her breasts met the V-shaped neckline.

He almost grabbed one of Aiden's crutches to steady himself as a sudden wave of lust nearly knocked him sideways. Where had *that* come from?

When Carmen finally straightened up, Caden asked, "How can you drive your police car with those girl shoes on?"

"I promise, the next children I sire are going to have better manners," Luke joked as he forced his eyes up to meet her face. But she must have been purposely ignoring him, because she wasn't looking his way at all. Instead, she was completely focused on his children and smiling. Was she wearing lip gloss? And where in the world had she been hiding all those inky black curls?

"I'm not working tonight. I'm having dinner with some fr—some ladies…with some lady friends." She waved at Maxine Cooper and Mia, who were already seated at one of the red vinyl booths. "What about you boys? I thought tonight was poker night?"

Had she remembered the invitation he'd awkwardly delivered yesterday? Probably not, since she still wasn't making eye contact with him. Maybe she was one of those females who related better to kids.

"It is. But it's Dad's turn to bring the food. Hey, you should come with us. It'll be more fun than sitting here and talking about lame girl stuff."

See. He wasn't the only one who'd just assumed she'd be more comfortable hanging out with the guys. But before he could say as much, his sister-in-law breezed into the restaurant.

"Aunt Kylie," both of the boys squealed before throwing their arms around her.

"Oh, you guys are getting so big!" Kylie said. "I've missed you two."

Luke felt a twinge of remorse. The boys had lived with her and Drew for several weeks and often stayed with them when Luke had to go out of town for trainings and recruitment seminars. But now that the couple had two newborns, Luke had tried to keep the boys away so they wouldn't become too much of a burden.

"Hey, Officer Carmen, in those boots, you're almost as tall as Aunt Kylie."

Luke had never really noticed the cop's height before, but in heels, she came to his chin. At least he guessed she would, if she ever got close enough to him to allow for an accurate measurement.

"My dad and Uncle Drew are both six foot four,"

Aiden volunteered. "But we might not grow as big as them because Grammie said our mom was only—how tall was Mom, again?"

It took a second to realize his son was asking him a question. Then it took another second to figure out what that question was. But after half a minute, Luke realized that he didn't have an answer.

How tall *had* Samantha been? She was on the shorter side, but he couldn't recall an exact height. He could remember the way she'd cried and threatened to leave the day he'd gotten his orders to go on a three-month overseas mission. He could even remember the defeated look in her eyes when she'd gone off that night to "have a few drinks with the girls." But lately it was getting more and more difficult to focus on the rest. No wonder Samantha used to accuse him of being emotionally unavailable.

Think, Gregson! Five foot four maybe? She was definitely shorter than the beautiful woman in front of him. He shook his head. What kind of man compared his dead wife to another woman? And what kind of father couldn't keep his thoughts in check when his children asked him such a simple fact about their mother?

"She was five foot four," he finally said while silently appealing for forgiveness in the event he was wrong. As well as forgiveness for the way he'd been too focused on Carmen's long legs.

His career and dangerous deployments had not only taken its toll on his family, it had also driven a wedge so deeply between him and Samantha that she'd turned to a bottle of vodka to ease her burdens. Just because he hadn't been the one behind the wheel on the night she'd died didn't mean he wasn't to blame.

Yet here he was, staring at Carmen, shamelessly taking in every glorious detail about her. The boys barely remembered their mother, and it was up to him to keep her memory alive for them—not get all hot and bothered about some incredible-looking female cop who had a soft spot for his kids. A flood of shame weighed him down, making him feel like he was closer to two feet tall.

Officer Delgado had her hands shoved into her jeans pockets and appeared to be reading the specials on the menu board several feet away. She obviously couldn't even bring herself to look at him. His toes flexed inside of his hiking boots and he clenched his jaw in disgrace.

"Well, you boys have fun at poker night," Kylie said, probably trying to lessen the awkwardness. "I figure I have about sixty-three minutes to get a bit of sustenance before Drew is gonna need me to head back over and feed the girls. So if I don't get some garlic knots and fettuccine Alfredo in me before then, there will be *three* very unhappy Gregson ladies."

Just then, a waitress walked up balancing four large pizza boxes and a couple of white paper sacks filled with Italian subs, and Luke had never been so glad for an excuse to get away. Even though he didn't think he'd be able to stomach a single bite.

"C'mon, monkeys," he said, peeling some bills out of his wallet and putting them on the hostess stand before taking the food from the server.

He maneuvered himself and the boxes out the door while the twins said their goodbyes and gave Kylie her usual three hugs, a ritual they'd started when she and Drew had been looking after the boys last year.

The cool air felt great on his overheated face, so he decided they would walk the few short blocks to Maxine and Cooper's apartment above the Sugar Falls Cookie Company.

He liked his cabin out in the woods, but Luke couldn't deny that the Victorian buildings lining downtown held their own appeal. If the boys didn't need so much space to run around, he'd gladly move in to one and try his hand at renovation. It might also shorten his commute. But then he'd have to interact more with the townspeople.

And, as he'd just displayed, he sometimes ended up looking like a complete ass when he did.

His life certainly hadn't turned out the way he'd expected. His training had conditioned him to always be ready to adapt and overcome—to put the mission goal first. However, just because he was ready to move on didn't mean he knew the direction in which he was headed. Maybe he should focus on figuring out a new mission instead of standing there like a tongue-tied fool who had no business lusting after his children's volunteer mentor.

They climbed the stairs and Cooper let them inside before grabbing the pizza boxes, carrying them to the white kitchen and opening them up on the counter. "Okay, kids, grab a slice and head on back to Hunter's room." Their host handed them each a paper plate then pointed to his stepson's bedroom down the hall.

Setting the rest of the food down, Luke said hello to Drew, who was pushing his sleeping daughters' double stroller back and forth, and to Alex Russell.

Luke was still somewhat new to the group, but Drew and Cooper had been stationed in Afghanistan together, and Alex coached both Hunter's baseball team, as well as Aiden and Caden's.

A knock sounded, and Coop grabbed a slice for himself as he walked to the door to let in the newcomer. Garrett McCormick had been Cooper's knee surgeon at the nearby Shadowview Military Hospital before opening up an orthopedic clinic in Sugar Falls after his discharge. Garrett had married Mia a few months ago—or had it been longer than that? Hell, Luke could barely manage to remember details from his own marriage, let alone all these dudes in Sugar Falls who seemed to be drinking from the same Kool-Aid cup.

"Sorry I'm late," the doctor said. "I had to drop off Mia's coat at Patrelli's. Her hormones are all kind of whacked out and she's been forgetting everything."

Alex, the only other single male present, covered his ears. "This is an estrogen-free zone, gentlemen. I do *not* want to talk about anything but baseball, beer and Clint Eastwood movies."

"Speaking of Clint Eastwood movies," Drew said as he piled food high on his plate. "Kylie and I were watching *Bridges of Madison County* the other day on TV and…"

A collective round of "No" and "C'mon" and "Yuck" went around the room. Someone threw a plastic pouch of red peppers at Luke's twin, who made the catch and then sprinkled some on his pizza.

"Actually, speaking of estrogen…" Garrett paused when he saw several packets of parmesan cheese aimed his way. "Wait, let me rephrase that. I was gonna say that when I stopped by Patrelli's, I saw Officer Delgado sitting with the ladies, and I hardly recognized her out of her uniform."

Luke's ears buzzed as the rest of the guys settled back into their seats. This was his chance to find out more about her without bringing too much attention to himself.

"Hey, Coop." Alex took a swig of beer. "I was meaning to ask what her deal was."

If anyone knew Carmen, it would be Chief Cooper, who was the woman's boss and had previously worked with her before as an MP when they were both stationed stateside. Luke held every muscle still, not wanting to miss the scoop and not wanting to grab the coach by the shoulder and tell him to back off.

There was that weird jealousy feeling again. What was up with that?

"What do you mean?" The police chief arched a brow. Yeah, what exactly *did* Alex mean? Was he interested in the female cop?

"I mean, does she do anything outside of work for fun? We have that intramural softball team we're trying to put together for the Western Idaho League and, well, I don't want to stereotype, but I've seen her out running and she looks like she'd be pretty athletic."

Luke let out the breath he hadn't realized he'd been holding.

"Oh." Cooper got up and brought a foot-long Italian sub sandwich over to the table. "I thought you were asking about personal stuff, which you know I can't give out."

"I'm not looking for a date, man," Alex said, and laughed. "I'm just looking for a shortstop."

"Why wouldn't you want to date her?" Luke felt

the words coming out of his mouth before his brain could process them. Just a second ago, he'd felt like shoving Alex's face into his pizza for even inquiring about Carmen. Now he was accusing the man of not finding her worthy enough of his interest. *Get back on solid ground, Gregson.*

"I didn't say I wouldn't date her. I said I wasn't looking for a date. Any date. At least not with anyone locally. Don't get me wrong, I know love and babies and rainbow-colored unicorns are running rampant in this town—" Alex looked pointedly at Drew, Cooper and Garrett "—but that pile of marriage crap you guys stepped in isn't for me."

"Amen." The word was out of Luke's mouth before he could stop himself. He tilted his beer toward Alex's and they clinked their bottles.

"Wait." Drew held up his hand. "Luke, I can't believe you just said that. Hello? You were married once, too."

"That was a one-time deal and it turned out I wasn't cut out for it, either." He didn't want to talk about Samantha or the shame-inducing lapse of forgetfulness he'd just had at the restaurant in front of witnesses. He didn't want to think about his marriage at all. He tried to keep all thoughts of that disaster hidden away in that footlocker in his mind and wasn't sure why everyone else on this planet suddenly wanted to bring it up.

"Don't you think you could be happy with someone again?" Garrett asked him.

A vision of Carmen's long hair framing her face, her glossed lips smiling at his sons, was the first thing that ran through his mind. But an occasional smile wouldn't be worth the inevitable heartache that would

result from getting seriously involved with a woman
again. Even if he could be happy, it wouldn't be long
before whoever he married wouldn't be.

"Nope, I'm good." He realized he'd responded a
little too loudly when he saw four pairs of doubting
eyes staring at him intently. "Look, the boys and I are
just settling into a routine and I'm still getting used to
the new job. My plate's pretty full right now. Besides,
every time I see her, she pretty much shuts down, so
I'm guessing she's in the same boat."

"Who?"

Luke looked up at Drew. "Uh, Officer Delgado?
Wasn't that who we were talking about originally
when Alex and Garrett brought her up?"

"Actually," Cooper said. "That was the conversation *before* it got segued into you not looking for a
relationship and Carmen not being interested in you."

"Did she tell you she wasn't interested?" Luke
raised his eyes like a hungry puppy looking for con-
firmation that there were no more pieces of pepper-
oni being thrown his way. "I mean, not in *me* per se,
but… Stop staring at me like that, you guys. I thought
we were talking about relationships and people not
looking for them."

"Oh, boy." Cooper retrieved a wooden game box
off the television stand. "We better deal the cards
while Gregson is still struggling to maintain his poker
face."

"I don't have a poker face because I don't *need* one
for this stupid conversation that you idiots steered
me into."

"Well, to answer your question," Cooper said, not
trying to hide his smirk. "Carmen hasn't said whether

or not she was interested in you or in any other man at this particular moment. But I *do* know that she's getting over some serious garbage she had to deal with in Las Vegas."

Luke remembered his sons telling him she had worked as a cop with the Las Vegas Metro PD before moving here, and he wondered what might've happened to cause her to leave such a large department, which probably had a lot more options for upward mobility than the tiny Sugar Falls Police Department. Maybe a cheating boyfriend on the force?

"Apparently she's taking out whatever the last guy did to her on men in general." Luke took another drink, holding himself back from asking for more information. "She treats us like we're all IEDs she needs to go out of her way to avoid."

"Hmm." His brother adjusted his gold-framed glasses. "She doesn't act like that around me."

"I've never gotten that impression from her, either," Garrett said, grabbing more pizza.

"Okay, so it's just me she can't stand to be around. Anyway, I'm not trying to get Carmen to like me." Oops. Had they heard Luke slip and use her first name?

"You could do worse," Drew said, and the other men chuckled. "In fact I've seen you do way worse back in the day. Maybe that's why you're so attracted to *Officer Delgado*. Because she isn't throwing herself at you."

Yep. They'd caught the slip.

"Don't try to psychoanalyze me, bro. Why can't I just be attracted to her since she's a beautiful woman who looks absolutely amazing in jeans and... Oh, shut up," Luke finally said when he realized Alex and Garrett were giggling behind their beer bottles like a couple of teenagers.

An infant let out a wail, and Luke wanted to kiss his sweet niece for coming to his rescue.

"I will say this for Carmen Delgado," Drew said. "She sure can put up with those adorable nephews of mine, so your battle to win her is halfway fought."

"Just a word of advice," Cooper said as he picked up plates to clear off the table. "You might want to take it slowly once you decide to finally bite the bullet and pursue her."

"Who says I want to pursue anything with her?" Luke would've kept arguing, but he saw all the men double over in laughter.

What he didn't see were his two blond curly-haired twins, standing on the other side of the door and giving each other a thumbs-up.

The following Saturday afternoon, Carmen pulled into the long driveway of the small riverside cottage she'd rented when she first moved to town. Her new home was on the southern border of Sugar Falls, and a little far from downtown, but she liked her privacy.

It was her third day off in a row, and she'd driven to the mall in Boise to stock up on makeup at her favorite department store. And to buy another pair of the jeans she'd been wearing Thursday night. It might've been just her imagination, but she could've sworn that Luke Gregson had been staring at her legs. At least until she'd knelt down to sign Aiden's pretend cast and he'd leaned over to stare at something else.

He was probably just curious as to how she signed her name or what kind of message she'd written. Still.

She'd experienced the heady rush of flattery for a split second. And, during that moment, she'd remembered that even though she'd had an emergency hysterectomy a year ago, the rest of her lady parts were still alive and well.

Then his words about his future children had turned her butterflies into blocks of concrete and her stomach had felt like lead when she'd tried to stand up.

She also recalled how pensive and eerily quiet Luke had gotten when Caden had brought up the boys' mother, the love of Luke's life. The man had completely shut down. His grief must be immeasurable to keep that kind of pain bottled up so tightly. A man that stuck on his dead wife was most likely *not* checking out Carmen in her civvies.

That was why she didn't do butterflies anymore. It was also why she shouldn't have wasted so much money at the mall earlier today.

As she parked her compact SUV next to her cottage, she caught sight of an empty canoe floating down the river behind her house. Uh-oh. That wasn't good. She hopped out and ran toward the bank to see if she could spot the riders who'd possibly fallen out of their boat. The river was fairly gentle here because of the bend a few hundred yards ahead, which tended to slow its current.

If the rowers had lost their craft farther up north, and closer to town, where the rapids were stronger, she might not see them for a while. But if they'd somehow tipped over near here, then they were obviously novices—most likely tourists—who would be in way over their heads when the flow picked up speed half a mile down.

Running up to her back porch, she grabbed a long rope, then raced to the water's edge. She didn't have to keep her eyes peeled for long when she counted three people in bright yellow-and-blue life jackets coming her way. She tied off the rope to a sturdy tree trunk along the river's edge and threw it across the water just as the trio floated by.

Her stomach tightened again when she saw who she'd just thrown a line to.

"Hey, Officer Carmen," a little towheaded boy called out as the more than capable Captain Gregson grabbed hold of the rope. Aiden and Caden were both holding on to their father, who was pulling them toward the shore.

"We lost our boat!" The other eight-year-old smiled in excitement, as though he'd lost another tooth, not a hand-carved, custom teak watercraft.

"How'd that happen?" she asked, trying not to stare at the sinewy muscles moving in Luke's biceps as he steadily alternated his grip, working his way up the rope.

Oh, to have those strong hands on her body, his arms flexing as he moved up her legs and…

Yep. Her lady parts were definitely still alive.

"You know, Delgado," Luke called out, sounding frustrated but not the least bit winded, "we might get to the shore faster if you helped pull a little bit. Boys, stop wiggling."

Duh. She'd been standing there salivating at the poor guy, as if he was a participant in a Navy SEAL wet T-shirt contest.

She grabbed on to the other end and put her own muscle into it. Lord, the man was as heavy as a tree trunk. Granted, he had the extra weight of his giggling and squirming sons to deal with, plus the river's current was starting to pick up speed, creating more resistance.

It took a few more heaves and the boys jumped off their dad and scampered up the bank, their interest diverted by some sort of amphibious creature in the shallow water. Luke took off his life vest and his wet shirt, and Carmen almost dropped to the damp pine-needle-covered earth below her.

Don't look, don't look, don't look.

She looked.

How could she not? The man had a torso that could've been sculpted from marble. He had muscles in places she'd didn't know humans were capable of having them.

"Do you have an extra towel by any chance?" he finally asked. Carmen jerked her head up, meeting his steady gaze, which she normally tried to avoid. She wished she'd tried harder this time. He was grinning at her, that little dimple winking in amusement, and she knew she'd been busted checking out the goods. But, man, were there some goods.

"I thought you Special Forces boys were used to getting things wet." Her hand almost flew up to cover her mouth. "I meant *getting* wet. In the water."

She had tried to be snarky, thinking that if she insulted his macho pride it would cover up the fact that she'd been eyeing him the way a barefoot woman would eye the shoe rack at a Nordstrom half-yearly sale. The resulting comment only made her seem even more like a sex-starved pervert.

"Yeah, well it's been a while since I've been exposed to anything that cold," he said. "Besides, with this unexpected heat wave, we wore shorts because

I didn't actually expect to end up in the river with the boys."

"Oh, my gosh! The boys." She turned to Aiden and Caden, who were standing ankle deep in the water, trying to catch bullfrogs and smiling through chattering blue lips. "Come on, kiddos. Let's go inside and get you in a hot bath to warm you up."

She jogged over to where the boys were and helped them get out of their soaking wet life jackets before steering them toward her cabin. She noticed Aiden's ACE bandage was gone and probably long forgotten. He didn't have so much as a limp.

"Uh, what about me?" Luke asked, still standing there, droplets of water trickling off the ridged planes of his abdomen. "Aren't you going to warm me up, too?"

She'd worked alongside men with oversize egos and the predispositions to flirt with a rock. But judging by the torch he was still carrying for his late wife, he was probably only making a dig at her for staring at him so blatantly. Even if he had been flirting, she knew better than to engage in any sort of banter that could lead to him thinking she was the type of woman who would welcome some tired line like that one.

"Simmer down, skipper. There's a stack of towels on the dryer in the mudroom. Help yourself while I get the boys in the tub."

"Maybe the water isn't the coldest thing I've been exposed to lately." He'd mumbled the words, but she'd heard the remark and shot him the withering look she'd perfected back when she was a Lance Corporal and the lone female in a platoon full of horny, young twentysomething-year-olds thousands of miles away from their wives and girlfriends.

She left him standing on her back porch and, after making sure the twins were in a warm bath and had something dry to put on afterward, she went into her room to change out of the jeans she'd been wearing when she'd stepped into the water to get the kids out of their vests. Come to think of it, her blouse was a little damp, too.

A few minutes later, when she padded out of her bedroom wearing cropped turquoise yoga pants and a plain white tank top, she found Luke in her living room, the towel he'd wrapped around his hips cinched low and tight. He was leaning against the back of her pink toile sofa; the only thing between his golden skin and the terry cloth material was the damp fabric of his shorts.

She sucked in her breath and felt her nipples tightening into hard buds.

"Nice, uh, outfit," he said. But his steel-blue eyes weren't looking her up and down. They were staring at the two points barely concealed by the thin white fabric of her tank top.

"You know what?" She crossed her arms over her chest, knowing the gesture was made to cover herself, as well as hold herself back from him. "I think I have a shirt around here somewhere for you to use."

She made an about-face and hustled to her bedroom where she stared at a pile of oversize T-shirts she'd accumulated over the years. Although many of the tees were gender neutral and came from a variety of tactical units and trainings she'd participated in, she was hard-pressed to find any sized double extra large, let alone double extra sexy. She finally settled on a dark green one at the bottom of the pile.

She'd been in such a hurry to get Luke covered up, it wasn't until she was standing in front of him with the shirt that she realized she should've grabbed one for herself instead of practically exposing herself in her skimpy tank top. Again.

"Hey, Officer Carmen," one of the boys said from behind her. She jumped away from Luke, as though her skin was completely on fire. "Where should we put our wet bathing suits?"

She blushed, thankful her back had been toward the bathroom door so the twins hadn't caught her reacting so physically to their father. She needed to get them out of there. All of them.

"Let's put them in the dryer so you can get them back on as soon as possible."

"That's okay," Aiden said. "I like wearing your stuff. It's soft and smells good."

Luke groaned when he saw his son in one of her oversize shirts. Apparently, he didn't like his son wearing a shirt that read "My Heroes Have Always Been Marines."

Well, it wasn't like she had kid-sized clothing just lying around her house. And the boys didn't seem to mind. In fact, Caden was still pumped from winning the round of rock-paper-scissors and getting dibs on the red one with a bulldog wearing a drill instructor hat.

"Do you guys need a ride home?" She handed over another T-shirt to Luke and walked toward the kitchen, trying to put as much distance between them as possible.

"No, but can I use your phone?" Luke asked. "Mine was in the boat when we tipped over and Cooper was supposed to meet us at the pickup point. I don't want him worrying if he sees the canoe floating by. He can probably swing by here and give us a lift."

"I'll just go make some hot cocoa," she said, then handed him her cell before walking to the kitchen. Normally, she found comfort in the sunny room with its blush colored walls, dark-stained wood cabinets and oversize white farmhouse sink. But today, the ninety square-foot space was closing in on her.

The boys followed her, and she could hear Luke making his call to Cooper and explaining where they were. She was just filling up four mugs when he walked into the kitchen, still wearing that damn towel. Too bad she didn't have any shorts big enough to fit him. Or a cabinet big enough to hide in.

He'd tried to squeeze into the shirt she'd given him, but it wasn't leaving much to the imagination. "Coop said he's still thirty minutes or so out. I hate to impose, but would you mind if I used your shower, too?"

"No." Was that husky voice hers? Maybe she was coming down with a cold. "Go ahead."

But before he could leave, Aiden spoke up.

"Hey, Dad. Officer Carmen kinda saved us, huh?"

"Well, she threw us the rope, but your old man could've done fine all on his own."

Macho jerk. Didn't they teach those SEALs how to be team players? She settled her fists on her hips and lifted her brow at him, as if to challenge otherwise.

"What? It's not like we were in any real danger. Just past your house is that old boat dock. We could've pulled ourselves out there and then walked back here."

"You know what?" Caden took a sip of his hot cocoa. "Choogie Nguyen told us there's this old Native American legend about a young girl who risked her life to save a brave warrior from the waterfall—you know that big one up the river? The one the town is named after?"

Luke's borrowed shirt was so snug Carmen saw his shoulders tense up underneath. He probably didn't like his children thinking he needed to be rescued by anyone.

"I'm sure lots of young girls had to risk their lives to save their tribe members," she said before sticking her head into her pantry, pretending to look for marshmallows. Couldn't the dryer go any faster?

"Your friend Choogie is a know-it-all," Luke told the twins. "People have been talking about that old wives' tale since I came up here as a boy. You guys know you shouldn't believe everything you hear."

Was big, tough Luke Gregson opposed to believing that a woman was capable of saving a man? Carmen was now intrigued. "What legend?"

"Oh, it's just some stupid nonsense that if a person rescues you from the Sugar Falls River, then you're going to fall in love and marry them." Luke waved his hand dismissively.

"Ew, gross!" Aiden cried, wrapping his arms across his face.

"You couldn't pay me enough money to get rescued by a girl and then hafta *marry* her." Caden flapped his loose red sleeves back and forth as if he could ward off the idea by making the international sign for stay back.

"No offense," Luke whispered to her. "The boys

are still in the stage where they think girls are yucky. Don't worry, kids. It's probably a big hoax some lonely woman made up to trick a guy into marrying her."

"Humph." Carmen looked at the ragtag trio standing in her kitchen, wearing her clothes. "More likely, it was the other way around."

Luke walked off to her bathroom and she leaned against the counter, drinking her hot chocolate and listening to the boys ramble on about other Native American stories and folklore. Oh, to be a kid again and to believe in all those glorious, adventurous tales. It was too bad people had to grow up and learn about the harsh realities of life.

Like the reality that no matter what some old legend might say, nothing could ever become of her and Captain Luke Gregson. Her brain knew it. And if she could just stop thinking about him lathering up his rock-hard torso in her shower, maybe the rest of her might realize it, too.

Chapter Four

Luke hadn't failed to notice that the shirt Delgado loaned him had the Marine Corps emblem on it. Or that it must've been made to fit someone much smaller than his six-foot-four frame. It wasn't his fault he'd ripped it when he took it off the moment he'd closed the bathroom door. Hell, he hadn't wanted to put the damn thing on in the first place.

Especially not after the way he'd seen her staring at him, first outside by the river, and then inside when he'd come in wearing that towel. Officer Delgado was finally looking at him as though he was a man and not a stain on her perfectly pressed uniform. And don't even get him started on how amazing she looked *out* of her uniform.

Seeing her flushed expression, his initial desire was to lift his arms up in victory. But his next desire had been to pull her into those same arms and show her exactly how much of a man he was.

Thankfully, his children had walked in on them and Luke was reminded of his commitment to being a better father. The boys had a special relationship with the female cop and they didn't need him interfering and messing things up.

So he'd grudgingly pulled the tight cotton material over his body and sat in that cozy, dainty kitchen, making small talk about old legends and trying to pretend that he was totally capable of being in the same room with a woman who'd surprised him by looking so damn…womanly.

Seeing her with her hair down at Patrelli's last week had been shocking enough, but then seeing her wearing that skimpy tank top in such an intimate, homey setting had melted his insides quicker than his hot cocoa melted the tiny marshmallows she'd sprinkled on top.

He picked the ripped shirt off the wooden floor and tried to fold it before placing it on the towel rack. Carmen Delgado seemed like the type of woman who took things seriously—her T-shirts, her job, her relationships. And Samantha's death had proved that Luke wasn't the ideal candidate for a serious relationship.

A chill reverberated through Luke's body and he stepped under the hot spray of the Roman shower, a luxury he hadn't expected her tiny cottage to have. Actually, there was a lot about Carmen Delgado he hadn't expected.

He stared at the array of bath products and specialty body washes before reaching for the turquoise—the most manly color option of all the bottles lining the tile shelf—shampoo and flipping open the cap to sniff it.

Hmm. Moroccan oil sure didn't smell too bad. As he squirted a large dollop in his palm, he caught sight of the price tag on the underside. Thirty-three dollars? For a twelve-ounce bottle of shampoo?

That seemed like a pretty big splurge for someone living on a small-town cop's salary. As he massaged the overpriced suds through his own short hair, Luke realized he'd used too much and worried that he might be depriving Carmen's long, thick hair of its expensive shampoo. Those dark silky curls were definitely worth the cost.

Luke turned the knob to lower the temperature of the spray. Fifteen minutes ago, he'd been a human Popsicle floating down the river and worried about developing frostbite on his appendages. But judging by the way his body was responding to the mere thought of Carmen in this shower washing her hair, he was getting way too heated.

And since he didn't want to go back out there and discuss girls rescuing warriors—or the fact that he'd needed rescuing in the first place—he took his time in the now-cool shower.

Let's see. What other interesting beauty products did she have in here? Coconut-mango sea salt scrub. He looked at the purpose and directions on the back of the glass jar, then rubbed the grainy texture between his fingertips. He'd spent enough time doing surf torture during trainings and maneuvers that he couldn't imagine why anyone would want to purposely cover their bodies in something most SEAL team members learned to despise.

Between the apricot mud facial exfoliant and the rose satin shave cream, Luke was hard pressed to find something he could wash his body with that wouldn't leave him smelling like a home garden show being held in a cotton candy factory.

He settled on something called Glacial Retreat Shower Mousse. Even the woman's bath gel was distant and aloof.

He shut off the water and didn't hear the boys yelling or otherwise causing any problems, so it was safe to say Officer High-And-Mighty had them well under control.

After he dried off, he wrapped a towel around his waist and took an inventory of all the small bottles of girlie potions organized neatly on the counter. He knew he should get back out there and check on the twins. Cooper would be here soon to give them a ride back to the cabin. But, besides the occasional family dinners at his mom's house in Boise, he hadn't been in a feminine domain since Samantha passed.

The familiar pang of guilt started low in his gut and he took a deep breath to try to tamp it down. Drew had told him plenty of times that he needed to stop feeling so responsible for his wife's death. That getting in a vehicle and attempting to drive when her blood-alcohol content was twice the legal limit was Samantha's mistake.

Yet, the reason she'd gone out drinking was *his* fault.

He looked at his reflection in the mirror over the sink and ran a hand through his wet hair, trying to pat down the cowlick that had always frustrated his mother, as well as any ship's barber whose chair he'd sat in. Drew would say that he needed to see a counselor, but Nana—if she were alive—would tell him to stop dwelling on the past and get right back into living for the now.

Speaking of the old gal, Nana would certainly have loved the assortment of beauty products on display in Delgado's bathroom. Luke saw a bottle labeled clarifying tonic and looked at the list of ingredients. He wondered how much it would cost to ship a case of this stuff to the guys on his team. It would be perfect for cleaning off that camouflage face paint they used during missions.

But it was no longer his team. Or his mission. His new team was the two eight-year-olds out there and his new mission was to be present. To provide them with a solid upbringing and unwavering love.

A lump formed in his throat and he shook it away. It was getting late and he needed to get the boys home and cook up some chow. He looked at the torn T-shirt and decided it probably wouldn't be very appropriate to go back out there in just a towel. His clothes were still drying, so that only left the short, silk robe hanging on the hook behind the door. Thank God it was yellow. Everything else in her damn house was fifty shades of pink. For such a tough Marine and cop, Carmen Delgado sure had a frilly girlie-girl side she seemed to keep hidden. The realization made Luke want to ruffle her feathers just a little. After all, what kind of self-respecting soldier surrounded themselves with all this fancy goop? It wasn't like she needed any of this junk, anyway.

As he stepped out of the bathroom, he called out, "Hey, Delgado, are you supposed to use the tea-tree-

and-avocado polishing mask before or after the cocoa shea-butter eye-firming cream? Oh, hey, Coop."

The chief of police and Delgado's boss was leaning against the back of the pink-and-white sofa. He was midsip from a mug of hot cocoa when he choked and then pinched the bridge of his nose, probably in an attempt to keep the liquid from shooting out of his nostrils because he was laughing so hard.

It took a lot more to embarrass Luke, though. "My clothes were wet. So it was either this robe or one of the eight hundred T-shirts Delgado keeps in her Marine Corps shrine collection. As a Navy man, I felt yellow and satin were better options." A little friendly rivalry between military service members was expected, so he didn't worry about Cooper taking offense.

"Nah, Gregson, I wasn't laughing at the robe. I was laughing at the fact that Delgado has something called cocoa shea-butter eye-firming cream."

"Why's that so funny?" Carmen crossed her arms over her chest, which she'd thankfully covered up with a bright pink hoodie. Luke didn't want anyone to witness his reaction to seeing her firm, round breasts on display again.

"Because, Delgado," Cooper said, still chuckling. "When I knew you in the Corps, you were one of the toughest MPs in our unit. And at the station, you're all business and no-frills. You don't even take creamer in your coffee. Therefore, I wasn't expecting your cottage to secretly house a day spa."

"Well, guess what. I like spas. I also like shopping and watching *Dancing with the Stars*."

"Wait, those are all girl things," Caden said before

looking at his brother and pretending to stick his finger down his throat.

Carmen rolled her eyes. "Well, I *am* a girl."

Luke tilted his head slightly to get a better view of her back curves in those yoga pants. He didn't think anyone would ever doubt that. Or that he'd ever be able to forget it.

Carmen would've laughed at the boy's skepticism if she wasn't already so annoyed with Luke's and Cooper's teasing. It wasn't her fault that nobody else in this town could see her softer side. Actually, that was fine as far as Cooper was concerned. She didn't want her boss to see her as anything other than a capable officer.

"Obviously, you're all female," Luke said, but she wondered if it really was all that obvious to him. "You just didn't strike me as a girlie-girl."

"Come on, boys," Cooper announced to the twins, who were all too pleased to borrow her shirts for an indefinite length of time. "Let's go wait in my truck while your dad thanks Officer Carmen for her hospitality."

"Aw, man. Why didn't you bring the patrol car?" Aiden asked.

"Because I'm off duty," Cooper replied as the twins followed him to the front door. "Besides, last time I let you ride in my squad car, I couldn't get my red-and-blue flashers off for a week.

Wait. Why was Cooper leaving her to deal with Luke by herself? What about the motto Leave No Man Behind? Did that suddenly no longer apply to her because she liked quality bath products and the color pink?

Maybe the chief sensed the uncomfortable attraction between her and Luke and wanted to distance himself from the fact that nothing positive could come from her lusting over one of his poker buddies.

At least the buddy in question was slightly more clothed than he had been twenty minutes ago—even if he did look absolutely ridiculous in her favorite yellow robe.

"Listen, Delgado. Coop's right. I should be thanking you for helping us out of the river and for letting us bombard your house like this."

Oh, Lord. That apologetic dimple of his should be illegal. When Luke smiled at her like that, she wanted to melt into a puddle at his feet. The man was probably used to women falling all over themselves just to get a chance to help him out. Which made her wonder how many females' houses he'd bombarded in the past, strutting around in nothing but a towel and steaming up their bathrooms with all his sexy masculinity.

She'd never be able to use her shower again without thinking of him in it. And she really loved her shower, damn him.

"It was no problem." She tried to sound casual. As if what she'd done for him was nothing out of the ordinary. "You and the boys needed help. I'd do the same for anyone else."

His grin shifted downward and he stood a little straighter. Nope, he definitely didn't like hearing that he wasn't special. Well, good. She couldn't have him thinking that he had any sort of impact on her.

"Of course you would, Officer Delgado. You're a regular Girl Scout."

She didn't know him very well, but she recognized sarcasm when she heard it. Why was he acting like the aggrieved party? She was the one who'd just had her whole world turned upside down when he and the boys capsized upstream from her house. Seeing them floating down the cold river had scared her, but then seeing Luke wet and in all his muscular glory had been a shock to her system. So then why was *he* so offended?

And why was he still standing in her living room?

A loud horn interrupted their standoff and he glanced at the open door before looking back at her. Why wasn't he leaving? "Sounds like the Chief is waiting for you, Captain Gregson."

"That's not Cooper honking." Luke rolled his eyes. "That's Caden. He always does three short blasts." Next, a long steady horn sounded. "*That* would be Aiden's honk. I better get there before Coop comes to his senses and kicks them out of the truck and we have to walk back to my cabin."

But he didn't make a move for the door. And then it dawned on her.

"Oh. Your clothes." She hustled over to the mudroom and opened the dryer midcycle. He was standing in her kitchen when she turned back to him. "The board shorts aren't bad, but the shirts are still pretty damp."

"Well, I can't exactly wear your robe home. I mean, I *can*, but I'd look pretty silly."

"Here." She handed him his bathing suit. "Put these

on and I'll go get you another shirt. Wait? What happened to the one I already gave you?"

"It was a little tight. I…uh…kinda tore it when I took it off in the bathroom. I'll get you another one to replace it."

"Don't worry about it," she called out over her shoulder as she headed back toward her room. "I have plenty more."

In fact, he could have his pick, as long as he got himself covered and out of her house. She searched her stack of T-shirts again, this time trying harder to find the biggest one. She started leave her room and then paused. She needed to allow him plenty of time to slip his shorts back on.

Normally, she was trained to run toward physical danger. It's what she was paid to do. But putting her emotions in the line of fire was a tactical mistake. Lord knew that if she walked in and saw him completely undressed, she'd be a goner. Or at least, more of a goner than she was now.

"Hey," he said, walking toward her bedroom doorway. She sucked in her breath and tried to focus her eyes on the yellow robe he was holding in his hand and not his bare torso. "The natives are getting restless out there."

"Right," she said, totally embarrassed to be caught standing there like a statue. It'd been a long time since she'd had a man in her bedroom and it had been even longer since she'd been near one that made her heart flutter this quickly. *Settle down, you traitorous butterflies.*

She threw him the T-shirt she'd been hugging to her chest. Her aim was a bit too high and he had to reach up to catch it. Big mistake. The muscles in his arm rippled into a well-defined bulge and stayed like that for way longer than necessary.

It took several blinks and an infinite amount of willpower to drag her eyes toward his face.

Whether his taunting smile was meant to mock her bad throw or to tease her for checking him out, Carmen didn't know. But she certainly didn't like it. Or her body's reaction to him. She needed to get him out of the house.

Instead, she let her eyes slide to the light pink puckered scar along his rib cage. "What happened there?" she asked.

He shrugged, absently touching the scar. "I was on a mission and our plane took a couple of rounds before we could jump. I was knocked back into the cargo door and…well, let's just say I was lucky enough that the surgeon who had to dig out the shrapnel was on board an ally ship and not working inside a POW camp."

"It looks fresh."

"It happened a few months ago. Right before I moved back to Sugar Falls. But you know what it's like to be a soldier. We all carry our battle wounds around with us."

Carmen tried not to move her hands to the scar below her abdomen. Her wound hadn't come from being a Marine, but she knew exactly what he meant.

"What's that right above it?" she asked. "A tattoo?"

"Yeah. After I left my SEAL team, I decided a scar wasn't enough. I needed a reminder of the most important moments in my life."

Carmen stepped closer and, while he kept his arm raised, allowing her to fully view his sculpted torso, she still had to stop herself from reaching out and tracing her fingers over the numbers. "Are they dates?"

"Yes. The first one is the day the twins were born. The second one is the day I started acting like a father."

Her head shot up to meet his eyes, but before he could explain the cryptic response, another honk sounded. He slowly brought his arm down, all the while staring directly at her face—which was mere inches from his. She could feel the warmth of his breath and she wondered if he could see her pulse thumping along her neck.

"I meant what I said, Carmen. I really appreciate you helping us out today." He backed away, pulling on the gray T-shirt as he went. She didn't respond, didn't say a word, until she heard the front door closing behind him.

At the sound of Cooper's truck roaring out of her dirt driveway, she finally allowed herself to move. She sat on the bed, then fell backward, laying her arm across her forehead. She could barely hear her own whisper above her pounding heartbeat.

"He didn't call me Delgado."

On a Thursday morning in late March, Carmen stood in the Snowflake Dance Academy, still surprised that there were so many women in this town who'd signed up for her cardio self-defense class. Most of them were sweaty—just like her—and a few looked zealously empowered after repeating the kickboxing moves she'd just shown them.

Mia had been right about offering a class like this, and Carmen was learning not to be so quick to make assumptions about the locals. Unfortunately, the mental preparation it'd taken for her to organize it hadn't been enough to steer her mind clear of its annoying habit of dwelling on Luke Gregson and his smug dimples.

It had been almost two weeks since she'd gone all googly-eyed on him while he stood there, shirtless in her bedroom. And it wasn't like she'd never seen a bare-chested man before. Hell, she grew up in a hot desert city with two brothers and a mess of boy cousins before joining the Marine Corps, where she was outnumbered by men four to one. But no man made her tingle like Luke did. Not even Mark, her ex-boyfriend and almost fiancé.

Carmen felt that tightening pang where her uterus should be. She'd heard of soldiers in the war who'd lost a limb and later experienced a sort of phantom pain, and she decided the expression was just as applicable to her.

Yesterday, she had talked to her mom, who'd delivered the not-so-surprising news that Mark and Carmen's cousin, Maria Rosa, were expecting their first baby. But the feeling of loss wasn't from missing her ex or from the awkwardness of her cousin being engaged to the man Carmen had once expected to marry. Her phantom pain came from knowing that she would never carry her own baby, that she was unable to give the gift of life to a child. That she'd never share the joy of parenthood with a husband.

"Okay, ladies." Carmen redirected her energy toward the thirteen women awaiting her next instructions. "Let's finish with some stretches and get you out of here."

She grabbed a mat, wanting to focus more on her tight muscles and less on her high-strung nerves, trying to remember one of her grandmother's favorite phrases about strength and character and being a woman. How did that old saying go? Maybe after this class she would call Abuela.

"That's it for today," she called out to the group, who gave her a polite round of applause. Carmen had recognized most of the local women, like Freckles, the older and sassy owner of the Cowgirl Up Café, and Elaine Marconi, who had told everyone about the twins knocking over Scooter Deets and the chips display. At least she hadn't completely banished them from getting slushies at the Gas N' Mart. Probably because the woman was always hoping for any juicy bit of gossip that came into her store.

Keep your friends close, and your enemies closer. No, that wasn't one of Abuela's sayings. Why couldn't she think of it?

Just then, Kylie Gregson handed her a cold bottle of water. "I thought I was a strong woman, Carmen, but you take strength to a whole new level."

"Se necesita un hombre fuerte para manejar a una mujer fuerte." Carmen's palm shot to cover her mouth. But the Spanish proverb was already out there. "Sorry, I'd been trying to recall something my grandmother always says and it just came to me out of the blue like that."

"I took Spanish in high school," Elaine Marconi volunteered. "And it does take a strong man to handle a strong woman."

Carmen wanted to grab the nosy woman's workout towel and cover the pink flush she felt climbing up her cheeks. Who'd asked for Elaine Marconi's translation, anyway?

"What strong man are we talking about?" Freckles wiggled the eyebrows she'd painted on to match her fire-engine-red-dyed hair. Carmen loved beauty products as much as the next woman, but she vowed to limit herself to face cream and lipstick by the time she reached the older waitress's age.

"I wasn't talking about a man," Carmen protested. "Kylie and I were just talking about being strong."

"Oh. Well, if anyone decides they want to talk about strong men, come on over to the café," Freckles said. "Post-workout smoothies and love advice are on the house."

Several other women laughed as they followed the self-proclaimed relationship guru and gathered their bags and water bottles. Carmen had heard that Freckles had been married at least four times, and rumor had it that she'd been driving up to Helena every other weekend to spend time with a former rodeo cowboy.

Unfortunately, before the crew of ladies could make it outside, Kylie added, "Oh, Carmen. Before I forget, Drew and I have been talking about doing a remodel of our bathroom and I need some construction advice. Luke told Drew about the shower he took at your place—"

"Hold the smoothies." Elaine Marconi was the first one to whip back around. "I wanna hear about Captain Gregson in Officer Delgado's shower."

"Luke Gregson could definitely be classified as a strong man," Freckles said to a chorus of feminine nods and sighs.

"No, it wasn't…he wasn't—" Carmen started, but Kylie jumped in.

"Officer Delgado was brave enough to rescue my brother-in-law and his sons a couple of weeks ago when their boat capsized on the Sugar Falls River." Kylie winked at her and whispered, "I got this," before hustling the busybodies toward the door.

But no matter how Kylie managed to spin the rescue story into a heroic tale of valor, there was at least one woman whose lips remained in an insolent smirk. On second thought, instead of using a workout towel to cover her blush, maybe Carmen could shove it in Elaine Marconi's gossipy mouth. Preferably before the woman spread rumors about her misadventures with the sexy SEAL all over town.

Chapter Five

"Thank God you're finally here, Captain Gregson," the school secretary said when Luke yanked open the front doors to Sugar Falls Elementary School. "Everyone's in the cafeteria with Caden right now, trying to talk him down."

Luke didn't bother with pleasantries or even a briefing of the situation at hand. Forty-five minutes ago, he'd been in the middle of a speech to several potential recruits at his office when he'd gotten the phone call from the school. He wasn't sure what had set his child off, but what he'd deduced over the phone from the frantic principal was that Caden had gotten upset during the weekly assembly and, instead of returning to his class afterward, had somehow barricaded himself above where most of the children would be arriving soon to eat their school lunch.

His heartbeat raced a mile a minute as Nana's Oldsmobile had labored just as quickly back up the mountain. But when Luke saw Officer Delgado's patrol unit—he knew it was hers by the "394" stenciled on the rear bumper—parked diagonally at the curb alongside a ladder truck from the Sugar Falls Volunteer Fire Department, he slowed himself to a light jog. At least there were professionals on the scene.

Hopefully.

When he entered the cafeteria, he saw the principal and a couple of lunch ladies wringing their hands and staring up at the ceiling. Luke followed their eyes and saw Caden, sitting on an exposed beam, tears in his eyes and his small arms wrapped tightly around the truss.

Officer Carmen Delgado, in her full gear and uniform, was calmly sitting beside an obviously distressed Caden, eating something that looked an awful lot like a chocolate pudding cup.

Luke's first instinct was to yell, but he didn't want to startle anyone when their balance looked precarious enough as it was. He saw a curly blond head sitting at a table with Scooter and Jonesy, the two old coots who ran the volunteer fire department. An aluminum ladder was propped up beside them, but instead of being on it, or actively trying to rescue his son, they were all sitting below it, eating pudding cups, as well.

What the hell was this? Some sort of pudding party?

"Aiden," Luke said when he made his way over to the trio. Make that a foursome, since his view of Nurse Dunn had been blocked by Scooter. "How'd your brother get up there?"

"I think he climbed up." Aiden pointed to where

some folding chairs had been stacked up high on a table. "But I didn't see him on account of our teacher made us sit separate from each other during the morning assembly because we were trying to teach some of the girls in our class how to make armpit fart sounds. But the girls aren't very good at it. Officer Carmen is, though. She can do a real good armpit fart when she isn't wearing her bulletproof vest."

Luke didn't exactly know what to do with that little bit of knowledge. "Aiden, do you know *why* Caden is up there?"

"I'm not sure, but I think he's pretty upset about something. He's been crying for a while and when the principal and teacher told him to come down, he wouldn't budge. I tried to go up and get him, but Nurse Dunn wouldn't let me."

The former Ski Potato Queen smiled at him, a dab of chocolate stuck to the corner of her purplish painted lips, and gave him a thumbs-up while keeping a tight grip on her plastic spoon.

"Anyway," Aiden continued, "they threatened to call you and the police but instead of making him scared, he seemed to relax a little bit and said he'd just wait up there for you and Officer Carmen to get here. All the other kids had to go back to class, but they let me stay and watch because Caden hollered real bad when they tried to make me leave."

"Okay." Luke ruffled his son's hair, thankful one of his children was safe and somewhat sane at this moment. "You stay down here. I'm going up."

Scooter stood to hold the ladder steady and Jonesy handed him a pudding cup. "You might want to take one of these with you."

Luke waved it off. "I'm not rewarding my son for this little stunt."

"Nah, that's for you," the man said, shifting a wad of pudding—or possibly tobacco—to his other cheek. "You might be up there for a while."

Great. Luke tucked the plastic container into the front pocket of his uniform and began climbing. When he got to the top, Caden turned his teary eyes toward Luke. "Hi, Dad."

"Hey, monkey," Luke said as he threw a leg over and straddled the beam. Just a few inches from Carmen's holstered gun. This wasn't exactly the way he'd imagined their next intimate meeting would take place. And ever since she'd stared at him so intensely in her bedroom, he'd been envisioning those a lot more frequently. "Care to explain to me why we're all hoisting ourselves up the rigging and there's no sail in sight?"

His son simply shook his curly head and stared straight ahead. Carmen looked at him and shrugged her shoulders, as though to tell him she had no idea what any of them were doing up here, either.

Her voice was soft and steady as she debriefed him. "We got the call and I offered to respond. I've been sitting up here with him for the past thirty minutes or so, but he hasn't said a word so far."

At least she was calm. Or giving one hell of a performance.

Maybe the guys below were right and they would be here for a while. He cracked open his pudding cup, then realized he'd forgotten his spoon. Carmen handed hers to him and he had to remind himself that this was about the least appropriate time to be thinking about the fact that the utensil had just been in her mouth, pressed against her tongue.

Hell. Luke rolled his ankles in circles—he hadn't been this high off the ground since the accident that had ended his SEAL career. He was officially horrible at this fatherhood gig. He could easily rescue a prisoner of war from a terrorist holding cell, and he could disarm almost any improvised explosive device, as well as manufacture and set one himself. Underwater. But he couldn't get his son to tell him what had upset him so much and he couldn't keep from having impure thoughts about the female cop trying to assist them both.

Drew was the psychologist and knew how to talk to people. His brother was the rational twin—the thinker. Luke was all about action. Act first and talk later.

"Caden, your daddy and I both want to help you," Carmen said. "But we can't do that until you tell us what's wrong."

"I don't want to talk about it." The boy sniffed.

"Okay, so why don't we talk about the assembly this morning, instead." Was this some sort of interview tactic? Because Luke didn't want to spend the rest of the day sitting on this rafter and shooting the breeze about routine school happenings. But he let the cop do her job. "Did you guys say the Pledge of Allegiance?"

"Yes," the boy mumbled.

"What about awards? Did the teachers give out any awards?"

"Not today. They just made a bunch of dumb, stupid announcements that nobody cares about anyway because they're so boring and lame and nobody will want to go anyway and you guys can't make me go."

Luke saw Carmen close her eyes and nod. Okay, so she was getting somewhere. Maybe.

"What kind of boring stuff will nobody want to go to?"

"That stupid dance. It's the worstest idea this school has ever had."

"But, Aiden," Luke started, "you love to dance. Remember when you took that hip-hop class at Mia's dance studio? She said you were a natural."

"But that's a different kind of dancing. One that we don't have to bring our moms to."

The realization cut through Luke's heart. He'd passed a flier on the office bulletin board but hadn't thought much about it. He should've been better prepared for something like this to happen.

"I'm not trying to add any pressure, Captain Gregson," the school principal called out, interrupting them just as they'd made some progress in figuring out what had the boy so upset. "But it's almost lunchtime and pretty soon we're going to have a bunch of hungry students headed in this direction."

"I'm not coming down until you cancel that stupid Mother-Son Dance," Caden yelled. Luke held up his index finger, trying to silently ask the principal to give them another minute.

"Aw, sweetheart," Carmen said, her soothing voice calm and understanding. "Now we get it."

"How are me and Aiden supposed to go when we don't even have a mother? We'll look stupid and everyone will make fun of us."

A tear floated on the tip of Luke's eyelid and he

looked up, trying to command it back into place. Even though they'd only been three when it happened, he'd known that Samantha's passing would leave his children with a huge void that he couldn't fill, and he was still learning how to be there for them as a dad. He had no idea how to be a mother to them, as well.

"You know, Caden, when I was a little girl, my school had a father-daughter chess tournament one year. But it was during the day and my dad couldn't take the time off work. So my mom made my oldest brother, Hector, take me."

"My dad used to not be able to take time off work, either," Caden said, adding to Luke's cup of guilt, which was in danger of overflowing. "But now he's around all the time and we get to be with him every single day. See? He's even here right now when he's probably supposed to be at work."

His son almost seemed proud of that fact, and since Nana had always taught him to focus on the positive rather than dwell on every mistake he'd ever made, Luke held on to that one tiny point in his favor.

"You're right, kiddo." Carmen nodded. "He *is* here right now. And he's doing such a great job of taking care of you and your brother, even though your mom's not here to help him."

"So you're saying I should have my dad take me to the Mother-Son Dance?"

That's not what she was saying at all. At least Luke hoped not, knowing full well he'd do whatever it took to make things easier on his children. Even if it meant dancing in a room full of boys and their moms. "Actually, I think Officer Delgado means you could ask one of your female relatives to take you. Like Aunt Kylie."

"Oh, yeah. Aunt Kylie'd probably go, right, Dad? She likes to dance."

"I bet she'd be honored if you asked her, monkey."

"Your dad will even let you use his cell phone to call her." Carmen's pointed tone was clearly not just a suggestion. "Let's climb down, so that you can do that."

His son now seemed eager to return to solid ground. Thank God.

"I'll go first," Luke said, since his foot was closest to the ladder rungs. "Then Officer Carmen can hand you to me."

"You don't want to just go down the way I came up?" Caden asked.

"No!" Luke's and Carmen's voices were in unison.

He motioned to Scooter and Jonesy and then waited for the older men to steady the ladder before holding out his arms for his son. Carmen easily picked the boy up and passed him over. Man, the woman was sexy and strong and a great voice of reason.

Luke squinted, catching a quick glimpse of the pattern between the top of her boots and the hem of her pants. Were those purple hearts dotting her socks? Yep, the woman definitely tried to keep her feminine side hidden when she was on the job. He held Caden in one arm and made his way down, trying not to look up and stare at her polyester-covered rear end above him.

Just then, several students entered through the doors, forming a line at the lunch counter.

"What's going on with your brother?" a kid asked Aiden. Luke recognized the boy as the twins' friend, Choogie Nguyen.

"He was mad that we don't have a mom to take us

to the Mother-Son Dance," Aiden explained, relishing in his role as information provider.

"Wait!" Caden, who was now standing on the linoleum floor, yelled loud enough to make everyone in the cafeteria freeze. "But that just solves *my* problem. What about Aiden? He doesn't have a mom to take him, either. We can't just share Aunt Kylie. We each need our own."

"I have two moms," Choogie said. "You can borrow one of mine."

"But your moms aren't my relatives." Caden shook his head. "I think we need someone who is a mom and a relative."

"You don't need a relative," Scooter said, throwing away the empty pudding cups as his partner Jonesy lowered the ladder. "Any gal will do."

"But what about a mom?" Aiden asked Choogie and the volunteer firefighters. "Does it have to be a mom?"

"Hey, Officer Carmen," Caden yelled, even though she was right beside him. "Are you a mom?"

"No," came her quiet reply. Luke could barely hear the woman, probably because his guilt was still pounding in his ears.

"Why not?" Choogie asked, like it was any of his— or anyone else's—business.

Her face paled and she looked at Luke before her eyes darted around, probably looking for an answer. But he was just as curious as the rest of the third-graders staring at them. She adjusted her leather duty belt. "Because I'm not married."

"Our dad's not married and he's still a dad."

"Listen, kiddos," Carmen finally said. "I think the

bottom line is that you can take any woman to the Mother-Son Dance. She doesn't need to be a relative and she doesn't need to be a mom."

"Oh, cool." Aiden pumped his fist in the air. "I call dibs on taking Officer Carmen to the dance, then."

By the time Carmen steered her patrol car into the parking lot near the Little League fields on Saturday afternoon, the baseball game was half over. But she was covering the afternoon shift for Officer Washington and she'd gotten a call to help a stranded motorist who, along with three college buddies, had attempted to do some off-roading in his Honda Civic. Luke Gregson was no longer the only man she'd rescued this month, but he was definitely the only one who'd made her nerve endings feel like someone had put a Taser to them.

It had been over a week since she'd been called to the school to help talk Caden down from the cafeteria rafters and almost three weeks since she'd pulled him and the boys out of the river. In the meantime, Kylie had tried to squelch the shower rumors, but Sugar Falls was a small town and just the hint of a potential scandal could turn her reputation and her relationship with the twins into a shredded paper target at the gun range.

Which was why she had no business getting any romantic ideas about Luke Gregson. Or promising Aiden and Caden that she'd come to their baseball game if they behaved and didn't get their names written on the whiteboard at school all week.

Really, after the cafeteria stunt, she'd thought winning that bet had been a sure thing. She'd never been more wrong.

She slammed her car door shut as if she'd just put all of her emotions under arrest and loaded them into the backseat to transport them to a faraway jail—out of her life and out of her mind. As she made her way toward the bleachers, she recognized the boy wearing the green jersey walking up to the plate, his blond curls peeking out from beneath his batting helmet.

"Hey, Officer Carmen," Aiden yelled out, making everyone in the stands turn to watch her approach. "Watch this."

She gave the boy a thumbs-up and stood near the bleachers instead of taking a seat among the moms and dads who actually belonged there. She told herself she didn't want to cause a distraction to the players or to the parents who were there to watch their children play ball. But, really, she didn't want to draw any more attention to herself. Or to the fact that she was on duty and taking her lunch break at the ball field because she'd been conned into it by a couple of precocious twin boys.

Last week, worried about their upset over the Mother-Son Dance, she'd shown up at their game after the first inning started and then hastily made a beeline for her car as soon as the teams began chanting their two-four-six-eight cheer signaling the end of the game. But it'd been easier to blend in last Saturday because she'd been off that day and didn't stand out like a sore thumb in her blue polyester uniform.

And at least she hadn't had Luke Gregson staring at her like he was now. She shoved her sunglasses into place, not wanting to make eye contact with the man.

Shouldn't he be watching his son? Aiden already had two strikes and Carmen was sure he'd get a third, but then he stepped into the pitch and swung with all his might.

Crack.

The ball flew toward center field. The kid on the opposing team was positioned under the fly ball, but ended up dropping the catch, causing Caden, the runner on second base, to make a mad dash toward third. Carmen glanced at Luke, who was acting as the third-base coach, and she had a brief flashback to that moment in her bedroom when he was holding his arm up and she was reading the inscription of the tattoo across his rib cage.

But this time, Luke's hands were waving in an attempt to convince Caden to stop running and remain on base.

Yet, Caden continued running and Carmen's heart froze when she saw the catcher, a sturdy girl who probably outweighed him by twenty pounds, holding the ball at home plate.

His brother had made it safely to second and was hollering out words of encouragement to Caden. Carmen's knees locked when she realized what the little daredevil was going to do. "No," she heard herself yelling.

Caden paused, and took a couple steps back. Thank God, he wasn't going to risk it. Then she caught the tilt of his small pink lips and as soon as the catcher threw the ball to third, the boy made a break for home plate. He slid in before the baseman could throw the ball back.

Which caused a domino effect as Aiden, who had

been perfectly content on second came rounding his way to third. Coaches from the red team began shouting instructions and kids from the green team began cheering while Aiden took advantage of the confusion and sprinted toward home, his slide not quite as graceful as his brother's.

"Safe!" the umpire, who looked suspiciously like Kylie's brother, Kane Chatterson, beneath that headgear and mask, called out.

Carmen let out the breath she'd been holding, relieved that both kids were uninjured. When the Comets won, the twins ran straight out of the dugout and toward her before they could even shake hands with the opposing team. Maybe it was unsportsmanlike conduct, but she couldn't help but be flattered.

"Did you see us, Officer Carmen?" Caden asked as he hurled his dirt-stained body at her. She caught him up in her arms and barely had time to brace herself before Aiden followed suit.

"Did you see us?" he questioned, as well.

"I did. You guys almost gave me a heart attack with that play." She set Caden down so she could give Aiden his hug. Then she said, "I think your coaches are waiting for you back in the dugout, though."

"Promise you won't leave," Caden said, and Carmen's heart felt like it had just slid into home, as well. But when she saw Luke motioning the boys over, she had to wonder if her heart was as overworked and tattered as the twin's white baseball pants.

"Well, I'm on duty and might get called out," she said.

"Then just don't leave without telling us goodbye."
She fixed the crooked brim of Aiden's hat, knowing

that the kid was busting her for sneaking away after last week's game.

But, really, what was she supposed to do? Stand there and make small talk with the rest of Sugar Falls, including their father? With the exception of that day in the school cafeteria, she'd been pretty successful at avoiding any conversation with Luke these past couple of weeks and, even though she knew it couldn't last forever, she was hoping to buy herself a little more time.

"I promise," she said, finally caving in. Was it even physically possible to tell these two boys no?

"We'll be right back," they shouted together before running to rejoin their team.

She smiled and said hello to a few of the parents trickling down the bleachers and toward the parking lot. After all, it was a small town and she was the only female officer in Sugar Falls, so many of them knew her, or at least knew of her.

Carmen wondered how many people really knew her at all.

But before she could ponder that lonely thought, Kylie Gregson, Luke's sister-in-law, made her way over, pushing the extrawide double stroller in front of her.

"Hey, Officer Carmen." Kylie, wearing a green team jersey, smiled at her. Even in a man's baseball shirt, the woman looked like a cover model. Some women gave off the feminine vibe without even trying. "The twins are so excited you made the game today."

Carmen's own smile was tentative, hoping the Gregson family didn't think it was strange that some Marine turned cop from Las Vegas was forming quite the bond with the two blond boys. "Are they always so reckless when they play?"

"When aren't they reckless? If it weren't for the strong family resemblance, I'd question whether any of the Gregson males were even related to my calm, good-natured husband. Especially this one."

Carmen hadn't seen Luke approaching behind her. His ability to show up unexpectedly and throw her off course was something she wasn't proud of, considering her career. She preferred to remain in control and unflustered at all times. Which was another reason she hadn't stayed after last week's game.

"Beautiful day for a ball game." Luke shot his dimpled grin at her before lifting up the sunshade on the stroller to peek in at his nieces. "Did they sleep through the whole game?"

"Yep." Kylie smiled proudly. "The Chatterson gene must've skipped a generation, because they've shown absolutely zero interest in baseball."

Luke laughed. "Don't let Kane or your father hear you say that."

Carmen had only found out recently that Kylie's dad was a famous major league coach. And everyone in town knew her brother, Kane, was on hiatus from his pitching career. In fact, he was hiding out from the mainstream sports media for reasons Carmen couldn't figure out, but she knew Kane's secrecy had something to do with the ball cap he sported at all times and the beard he'd recently shaved off. But Kylie and Luke both smiled at her as if she was in on the joke.

"We're back, Officer Carmen," Aiden said as the twins approached them. The strap of his bat bag was looped over his wrist, allowing him to drag his gear behind him while his hands were busy trying to open the plastic bottle of fruit-punch-flavored Gatorade. "Me and Caden decided you're our good luck charm."

"Yeah," Caden said around a slice of orange from his after-game snack bag. "Every time you show up at our game, we play better."

Her? She was nobody's lucky charm. And being from Vegas, she was well versed in what constituted good luck. "I don't know about that."

"No, it's true. Remember two weeks ago when I was pitching and the other team got three walks in one inning?"

"Yes." Carmen nodded. "I was here for that, which means maybe I was bad luck."

"Nah. You had to run over to the playground area to help get Choogie's little sister unstuck from the monkey bars. So you weren't really watching. But after you came back, I threw five strikeouts that game."

She raised an eyebrow at Kylie, as if to say *help me out here*. Carmen didn't want the boys thinking she had anything to do with how they played the game. But the redhead shrugged her shoulders. "Don't ask me. The girls both had colds so I wasn't here."

"Well, what about when Aiden hit that foul ball in the sixth inning last week?" Carmen asked. "The one that hit Marcia Duncan's new Smart car and cracked her windshield? That wasn't very lucky." Pointing out an innocent kid's mistake left a bitter taste in her mouth. But she couldn't very well have the twins thinking she had supernatural powers. They needed to realize that they played well all on their own.

"You saw that?" Luke winced. "But you were off getting some nachos when that happened."

"How'd you know where I was?" she asked, then tried to erase the surprised look from her face. "Besides, I was watching them from the snack bar area. Anyway, even if I hadn't seen it, I had to take the accident report on it so Mrs. Duncan could file a claim with her insurance company."

"But we couldn't see you 'cause you weren't near the bleachers," Aiden said. "So it doesn't count."

"Did you tell Mrs. Duncan that she looks funny driving around such a teeny tiny car?" Caden added. "Remember those clowns we saw one time at that rodeo in Grangeville, Dad? We probably did her a favor by wrecking that thing for her. So maybe you're good luck for us *and* for big ol' Mrs. Duncan."

"Boys," Luke finally interrupted his sons. "I think you're making Officer Delgado uncomfortable with all this good-luck talk."

So they were back to Officer Delgado again. Almost four weeks and she was still trying to forget the way her first name sounded on his lips. She should've been relieved. Instead, she felt her own lips turn down and her blood heat up in annoyance.

"Oh, look," Kylie said, and pointed out a white van in the parking lot. Recorded organ music was coming out the speaker mounted to its roof. "There's an ice-cream truck. C'mon, boys. I'll buy you guys a Popsicle to celebrate your win."

The woman winked at Carmen before pushing the stroller away, her nephews trailing behind her. Which left Carmen in the exact position she'd successfully avoided for the past twenty-three days and twenty-two hours.

Alone with Luke Gregson.

Luke had seen her the moment her patrol car pulled into the parking lot. Hell, if he was being honest with himself, he'd been trying to catch glimpses of her in town all week. Or at least since he'd seen her sneaking away from the stands at the bottom of the ninth inning last Saturday.

In the school cafeteria, she'd been all business. And even though his sons saw her every Tuesday afternoon and they'd shared a rafter and a pudding spoon, he hadn't made any attempt to talk to Officer Delgado alone since that heated moment in her bedroom.

Had he been inappropriate in any way? After Samantha died, Luke had lost all interest in the rules of attraction. Still, he'd gone over the bedroom conversation and the sequence of events in his mind several times since then. But the only thing that remained the same was the way she looked, standing there by her bed in her tight athletic pants and body-skimming pink hoodie. Or the way she'd stared at his bare torso, her full lower lip caught between her straight white teeth.

Of course, it didn't help that he couldn't forget the smell of her, probably because the scent from her shampoo had lingered in his own hair for several days—despite the fact that he'd washed it repeatedly.

"It's funny what they get into their heads," she finally said, drawing his eyes away from her tight no-nonsense bun.

"What who gets in their heads?"

"The boys. Thinking that I'm some sort of good luck."

"Oh, that," he said, then used the toe of his sneaker to push on the dirt beneath his feet. *Get back on solid ground, Gregson.* "The twins mentioned it last week, too. Not that I believe in any of that, but they'd both struck out before you got here today and Caden missed an easy catch at first base earlier in the game. I don't know if it's self-fulfilling prophecy or what, but they're more convinced than ever that unless you're at their games, they won't play well."

"But that's silly," she said.

"Try explaining that to a couple of eight-year-olds. Actually, nine-year-olds as of this Friday."

"Oh, that's right. The boys mentioned you were throwing them a big birthday party since it's a half-day at school."

"Did they invite you?"

"I'm pretty sure they invited half the town, Luke."

He smiled when she said his name, even if she had ducked her head as soon as she'd said it. Was Officer Always-in-Control embarrassed?

"Well, they didn't invite Marcia Duncan," he said, trying to make a joke to keep her talking.

"I'm pretty sure that after the windshield incident and what happened last week in the meat department, Mrs. Duncan is all too happy to *not* be attending their party."

Luke felt the familiar sensation in his gut. "Oh, no. What happened?"

Carmen sighed. "I took them to Duncan's Market to get some fruit after school since things are still a little tense over at the Gas N' Mart after, well…you know. We started out in the produce section, but then I turned to talk to Mayor Johnston and next thing I knew, I found them by the beef display case pretending that the ground round on sale was actually some sort of brain science experiment and… Well, my freezer at home now contains quite a few packages of hamburger with finger indentations poked through them."

Luke would've groaned at his children's antics if she hadn't just reminded him of her home, and her freezer, which was in her kitchen. Where she had stood in that skimpy little top that outlined the shape of her—

"Hey, Dad." Caden's voice interrupted his train of thought just in time. "We got you a choco-freeze bar."

"And we got a strawberry shortcake one for Officer Carmen," Aiden added.

"Where's your aunt Kylie?" Luke asked.

"One of the babies started cryin' so she said she had to leave. But not before she agreed with us about Officer Carmen being our good luck charm." Here they went again.

"Yeah, she even paid for yours, Officer Carmen, and said there's more where that came from if you keep showing up for our games. Maybe she'll even buy you some nachos at the snack bar next time so that you don't miss a thing."

"That's awfully nice of your aunt." Carmen unwrapped the melting treat. How long had they been hanging out by the ice-cream truck? "But nobody needs to buy me food to keep me around."

"Oh, good, then you'll be at our next game. And we

don't need to buy that dulkie de—what's that flavor called again?" Caden looked at Carmen.

"Dulce de leche," she said, her accented pronunciation making Luke think of other things her tongue might be capable of.

"Yeah. *Dulce de leche* cake for our birthday party. That's Carmen's favorite kind," Caden told his dad. "We can just have regular chocolate with chocolate frosting and you'll still come."

Was she really coming to the birthday party? The one he planned to throw at his cabin? The one he'd had to promise five nights of niece babysitting if Drew and Kylie would help him organize the thing? In the back of his mind, he knew that it would just be a simple event for kids—a little cake, maybe a piñata—but he still was dreading his first foray into hosting anything more than a family cookout. Surely, she had better things to do on Friday night then hang out with some kids, their clueless dad and a store-bought chocolate sheet cake.

He wanted to ask her all those things, while not giving away any indication that a small part of him was hoping she'd be there. But the boys were too busy describing all the toys they'd written on their gift wish lists.

While she nodded along with them, indicating she was listening to their rambling chatter, Luke had the feeling she was staring right at him, those damn sunglasses preventing him from reading her full expression. Did she not want to come to the party? Was she looking to him for an out?

It was bad enough that his children had already guilted her into showing up for their next baseball game. She wouldn't be the first woman who needed a break from the twins. And if he wanted her to stick around—strictly as a mentor to the boys, nothing else—he needed to tell her she was off the hook, but she spoke before he could.

"I'm sure you guys don't want some boring girl like me at your party. You'll be so busy with all of your friends, it won't matter that I'm not there."

"But, Officer Carmen, you're one of our bestest friends. Of course you have to be there." The sad, Popsicle-stained faces stared up at her from beneath the brims of their green caps.

If he wasn't used to the twins making that same expression every time they wanted to stay up past their bedtime or eat pancakes for dinner, he almost would've felt sorry for the little rascals. Almost. But he'd invented that helpless look when he'd been their age and needed to get out of trouble—which was almost every day.

He told himself that the only reason he didn't tell the boys to knock it off was because she was such a good influence on his children and he wanted them happy. Then, when he heard her exhale a deep breath and saw her shoulders relax, he knew she was close to giving in.

Which meant he was getting closer to doing something about this growing attraction to her. Something that they would both surely regret.

Chapter Six

"I know I said I'd help you with the party, Luke." His sister-in-law raised her voice to be heard over the two fussing babies on her end of the line. "But the twins are teething and I'm in the middle of tax season."

Luke looked down at his cell phone, wishing he'd sent the call to voice mail and kept on making dinner. But then he remembered that he was no longer hiding behind his former job title. He was now a full-time a dad. An impulsive one who didn't always make the best decisions, but a dad nonetheless. If he could parachute into enemy territory on covert operations, he could tackle the simplest of domestic duties without fear.

In his defense, though, he wasn't dealing with the simplest of domestic duties. He didn't know how to throw a birthday party for nine-year-olds. He'd missed their last two birthdays and wanted to make sure that this year was beyond memorable for Aiden and Caden.

"But don't worry," Kylie continued. "I'll email you the lists and Drew and I will be there on Friday to help set up. And I already recruited…to go get…with you."

"Kylie, I can't hear you." His nieces were getting louder on the other end of the line and the timer on his stove was going off. "What lists?"

"Oh, you know. The guest list and the food lists and the games and prizes list."

"Games and prizes? We need a list for that?"

"Only if you don't want the kids to get bored and stage a piñata mutiny. Carmen said that happened at one of her cousin's birthdays and it's not pretty when you get that much sugar into forty children half an hour after their parents drop them off."

"Carmen? Did you say Carmen?" He pushed a button above the stove and finally got the timer to stop beeping. "And what was that last part about forty kids? That's not what's on the guest list, is it?"

"Luke, focus. I ran in to Officer Carmen today when I was downtown, and she said she was off work and could help you shop for supplies on Thursday after her kickboxing class. She has a huge family back in Vegas and said they average three birthday parties a month. I'm leaving you in good hands."

In good hands? As in Carmen Delgado's good hands? While Luke had to admit that the cop certainly had nice, capable hands—probably scented with some sort of fragrant specialty lotion—Luke didn't know if that would be asking too much. After all, she already helped him out with the boys through that mentor program, and if they worked on the party together, their sudden closeness might give the wrong impression.

Not that he wouldn't welcome the help, but did he really want the rest of the townspeople getting the idea that she was some sort of surrogate mother?

And was she? He was pretty sure that even if she wanted to play mom or big sister or whatever to a couple of boys, she wasn't particularly eager to step into the wife role.

Whoa. Where had that idea come from?

"Why would Carmen agree to help me?" Luke asked instead.

"Because she loves the twins and wants them to have a fantastic party. And because I bribed her with an all-expenses-paid trip to the Cove Spa in McCall." Another burst of crying interrupted them and he barely heard Kylie's voice say that Carmen would be by tomorrow morning with the lists before the call was disconnected.

There was no way he could spend the whole day with Carmen Delgado. She would be all uptight and he'd be on edge trying to get her to loosen up, and then she'd probably throw those so-called good hands up in the air in frustration and never want anything to do with him or the twins again.

Maybe his mom would drive up from Boise and help… But she'd already been responsible for the birthdays he'd missed and had hosted her share of kid-themed parties in the past. Nope, he didn't want to trouble her with something he should be able to handle.

After all, he was a captain in the Navy, the head of recruiting for the entire West Idaho region. He was handling everything else in his life just fine. For the most part.

Luke looked down at the pan of ground beef he'd been browning for dinner. Why was it smoking? Damn. He'd forgotten to turn off the flame after the timer went off. He slammed the skillet on the back burner and opened the window over the sink.

Just when he thought he'd been doing pretty well in the dad department, another setback came his way. He stared at the bits of charred meat, hesitating to call the twins over to the table.

A flashback from his boyhood hit him and he remembered his nana cooking one time when he'd spent the night at her house. She'd put a frozen pizza in the oven and then turned on the Country Music Television channel, calling an eleven-year-old Luke into the living room to do the "Boot Scootin' Boogie" with her. He'd thought dancing was for girls, but the cowboys on TV didn't look all that girlie. Plus, Pioneer Days was on the calendar at school soon and his teacher had warned the students that they'd all have to learn to square-dance as part of the festivities. So after a small amount of convincing, he'd line danced with Nana, learning the Cowboy Cha Cha and the Eighteen Step. By the time they'd mastered the Watermelon Crawl, Nana's smoke alarm was shrieking at full blast.

She'd tossed the burned pizza in the trash and told Luke, "It's not the food we eat, it's the company we keep that makes a good meal." Then they'd made root beer floats for dinner and watched reruns of *Hee Haw* until he'd fallen asleep on her sofa.

Sure, the cheesy beef and macaroni he'd made tonight was a bit on the overdone side. But he'd had way worse meals in bunkers and tents around the world. What mattered was that he was here with his children and that he was providing for them. They were a family—and they were together.

And he was about to throw them the best damn birthday party Sugar Falls had ever seen.

Carmen couldn't believe she'd agreed to help with this birthday party. Actually, she pretty much would've agreed to anything that made Aiden and Caden Gregson happy, but it was their aunt who'd convinced her.

When Kylie ran in to her outside of Domino's Deli yesterday, the woman had been panicked that the birthday party would be a complete failure since she was too busy to take care of the last minute details herself. And it hadn't taken much begging on Kylie's part to convince Carmen to step up to the plate.

Truly, Carmen would've done it for free. But now, as she navigated her SUV over the ruts in the dirt road leading up to the Gregson cabin, she decided that working side by side with Luke today was enough of an emotional chore to earn a relaxing trip to a day spa.

She put the car in Park and turned down the radio station she'd been listening to. Her appreciation for George Strait and Garth Brooks rather than Jenni Rivera and Intocable should've been her first clue that she didn't fit in well with her own family. She loved them and knew they loved her, but she'd always been destined for different things.

However, today wasn't a day to be thinking about her past and all the things she couldn't change.

She gathered the lists she'd printed off earlier this morning and exited her car. As much as she had wanted to wear a dress or something more feminine to remind Luke that she was more than just a cop, she also wanted to be comfortable with all the shopping and hauling that they were going to be doing today. So she'd settled on the low-waisted jeans she'd been wearing that night at Patrelli's—the night he'd said he wanted more children—and a black V-necked sweater. Although she did add her metallic purple ballet flats at the last minute, just to soften things up.

She ran her fingers through her loose curls, debating whether she should've pulled her hair into a ponytail, then wondered what she was even doing on his front porch in the first place. Before she could second-guess herself, she knocked on the door, taking a slight step back when Luke flung it open.

"Hi," he said, somewhat winded and twisting a dishcloth in his hands. The sleeves of his blue thermal shirt were pushed up to his elbows, his forearms slightly wet with soap suds. "I was just trying to get the dishes done and a load of laundry going before you could see what a wreck this place is."

He and his dimples stood back, allowing her to step into the cabin. It wasn't dirty, but she could definitely tell that a couple of creative and high-energy boys lived here—along with their high-energy dad, who could charm the socks off most of the ladies in Carmen's growing kickboxing class.

"It's not a wreck," she said, thinking back to some of the meth houses and condemned buildings she'd made arrests in when she'd worked in Vegas. "It just looks…lived in."

"That's one way to put it." His smile deepened and she found herself a little disappointed to see him pull down his sleeves. The guy's forearms really were amazing, as was the rest of his upper body. "So what's on the party planning agenda?"

She jumped at the opportunity to launch into professional mode. Controlling mode. "I figured we could pick up the decorations and most of the groceries today. The rental company will be by tomorrow to set up the chairs and tables and I can pick up the cakes in the morning on my way over here to help prep the food." She saw his eyes glance down toward her breasts but then realized he was probably looking at the papers she was holding against her chest. "Oh, and Kylie emailed me these."

She thrust the papers at him, and his fingers brushed hers as he took them out of her hands. She felt that zappy feeling again and tried to remember her stun-gun training. One small tingle of current wouldn't hurt, but a full force of electrical shock could do some serious damage. She made a mental note to avoid any more accidental physical contact with him.

"Why do we need to rent tables and chairs?" he asked before flipping to the page with the guest list. "What the...? Is this all the people invited?"

She wanted to laugh at the surprised look on his face and felt just the slightest twinge of guilt for her growing desire to overwhelm him a bit more. "No, those are only the people who can make it."

"But there's gotta be over a hundred people on this list!"

"Actually, there's one hundred and fifty-two if you don't count the girls from the Junior Jazzette dance troupe. Since school gets out early, they have a late matinee performance at the Remington Theater tomorrow and Mia doesn't know if they'll be done in time for the party."

Carmen caught a movement on the hardwood floors and saw Luke's bare toes do an odd flexing thing. Man, even the guy's feet were muscular and sexy.

"Are there even one hundred and fifty-two people living in Sugar Falls?" he asked sarcastically.

"Oh, come on, Captain Gregson. Don't tell me that a big, tough Navy SEAL is afraid of a simple gathering."

He looked up. "It's not the large group I mind. It's the being responsible for entertaining them all that I wasn't expecting. I told the boys last Monday that they could invite a few friends, but this is ridiculous. How did they even get the chance to talk to so many people in such a short amount of time?"

She showed him the printout of the online invitation. "I was under the impression you'd sent this to everyone since it came from your email address. But, knowing the twins, I probably shouldn't have assumed anything."

"'Come one, come all?'" He read aloud. "Did they really put that on the e-vite?"

"Luke, I'm starting to see where Caden gets his flair for drama. It's really not that big of a guest list. In my family, anything less than two hundred people isn't even considered a party. We call it Sunday night dinner. My cousin Maria Rosa had three times that many to her *quinceañera*." Of course, Maria Rosa, being younger by six months, had always tried to go out of her way to outdo her older cousin.

"You mean this is going to get worse every year that they get older?" Luke's face paled.

She finally laughed out loud. "Relax. Just think that with twins, you're getting two birthdays for the price of one."

"What a bargain. So where do we get enough food to feed all these people? I've been too nervous to step foot in Duncan's Market since you told me about the boys getting eighty-sixed from there."

"There's a big party-supply store in Boise, so I figured we'd go there first. Then we can swing by Costco after that."

"Swing by Costco?" He lifted one eyebrow. "I haven't been to a bulk warehouse like that since the twins were in diapers. Samantha used to say that we should've bought stock in that place. And in baby wipes."

The butterflies in her tummy had just turned into hornets. She wished she didn't feel so stung by the sudden mention of the twins' mom. Carmen had absolutely no claim to Luke and shouldn't be even the slightest bit jealous of his love for his late wife. Yet, some of her humor was lost by the reminder that not only would she never be buying diapers with a husband, the one man she was attracted to was in love with someone else and, therefore, on the shelf.

"Well, then, get your wallet ready, Captain." She retreated into her default professional mode. "Judging by Kylie's list, you're going to be spending a lot of money today."

He grabbed on to his back pocket dramatically, as if he could protect his billfold, and she tried not to think of what it would feel like to cup her own hand against that perfect curve of his jeans.

"Okay, sailor." She yanked the lists out of his hand and turned toward the door. "This ship needs to sail if we're going to get all this done before the boys get out of school."

"All right. As long as I can steer the ship." She heard the jangling sound of his keys.

"No way," she said. "We have a lot to buy and my car's bigger."

"I'm starting to think you have control issues, Officer Delgado."

"I'm a woman in a male-dominated field. I'm supposed to have control issues," she said.

"Not with me, you're not."

"Listen, Gregson. There's something I've learned about the two types of men out there. There are the ones who don't like a woman being in a power position. And the ones who think they like a woman in a power position, but when they end up finding out what that entails, they can't handle it."

"Well, allow me to introduce you to the third type of man," Luke said, pointing to his chest. "The one who's a team player. Gender doesn't matter to me as long as the mission gets accomplished. And this mission requires a roomy Oldsmobile."

"I'm sure Nana's car is a real beaut and that the ladies are all lining up for their turn to be squired around in it. But my car has way more space. If we fold down the seats, you could even lay down back there. It'll make for a better ride."

His gaze dropped to her waist and there was no mistaking the way the warm color rose along his neck. Or the fact that gender *did* matter to him when he'd misconstrued her suggestive words.

"I meant since you're so big and… Oh, never mind,"

she muttered, turning away before he saw her matching blush. "You can drive."

"I don't know why we had to get two piñatas," Luke said as he tried to shove the papier-mâché-covered cartoon character into the backseat of Nana's Oldsmobile. He sure hoped his children enjoyed this birthday, because after filling two shopping carts full of decorations and favors at the party-supply store, this was the last one he was willing to throw.

"We got two piñatas because you have two children," Carmen explained as though Luke didn't know exactly what it was like to have twins. Hell, he'd grown up as one himself. But his parents had been on a budget and they'd been smart enough to make sure their children didn't invite that many people to their parties. Plus, Luke hadn't had access to online invitations back then.

"Aiden wanted a superhero theme," Carmen continued as she piled bags onto the seat. "And Caden wanted ninjas. So we're getting two of everything."

"But we haven't even made it to Costco yet. How are we going to fit everything in here?"

"You're the one who wanted to bring the Nanamobile." He looked up just in time to see her roll her eyes. "I offered to drive, remember?"

Luke remembered all right. The minute she'd suggested putting the seats down in her car so he could lie back there and have a more comfortable ride, he'd made the mistake of looking down at her athletic body and envisioning the exact type of ride he'd prefer to enjoy with her.

Then she'd made an about-face and headed straight

for the driveway, her coolness serving as a reminder that Luke had no business getting involved with another woman, let alone the controlled female cop. The drive to Boise had been awkwardly silent until they'd finally passed the Shadowview Military Hospital and Luke couldn't stand the quiet any longer. He'd turned on the radio, the old dial stuck on a country music station. By the time they'd made it to the party-supply store, Carmen didn't seem as tense and had naturally fallen into her element by taking over the list of what they'd need for the party.

Now he watched her yank her arm out of the way just in time to slam the car door closed against the tumbling bags. He doubted they really needed paper napkins in five different colors, but every time he'd expressed an opinion about buying so much stuff, she would point out the item on Kylie's never-ending list of things to make sure this was the biggest kids' birthday party the town of Sugar Falls had ever seen. Carmen Delgado must've been one hell of a Marine with the way she followed orders.

He got into the driver's seat and glanced at the sushi restaurant across the street. Was it too early for lunch? His stomach was telling him it wasn't, but his no-nonsense passenger's professional demeanor was telling him that going out to lunch—just the two of them—might seem a little too date-like. And he didn't want her thinking he was trying to come on to her. Instead, he put the car in Drive without saying a word.

They were on their way to get groceries when he saw the sign for the giant toy store and a little light inside his head clicked.

"Man, I totally forgot," he said as he hit his turn signal. "I haven't even gotten the boys their presents."

Carmen looked at her watch since the display clock in the Oldsmobile was stuck indefinitely on 8:56. "It's already eleven hundred hours and you need to be back in Sugar Falls in time to pick up the twins from school."

"I'm their dad. I can't *not* get them something for their birthday. Besides, I'm sure they'd rather have new toys than—" he picked up the grocery list sitting on the bench seat beside him "—two pounds of hummus. Who's going to eat all that, anyway?"

"Oh, fine," Carmen responded with a sigh. "But let's try to get in and out in under twelve minutes."

Twelve minutes? Did the woman think they were running some sort of covert op here? Maybe they needed to synchronize their watches or wear radio headsets to communicate throughout the assignment. But instead of making a sarcastic comment to Officer Controlling, he revved the engine of the Oldsmobile and pulled into a parking space in front of Toy Town, barely missing the curb. Nana would've been proud.

Carmen grabbed her purse, a purple leather satchel that matched her dainty shoes, and Luke followed her to the entrance, thinking he still wasn't used to seeing her with so many feminine accessories. She even had large gold hoop earrings on and several delicate bracelets tinkling against her wrist.

Not that he was paying attention.

"I used to love this place when I was a little girl," she said, slowing her stride as they walked inside. Her chocolate-brown eyes were enormous, taking in all the colorful displays of the latest toy crazes. Luke couldn't imagine someone as proper and as stiff as Carmen ever being a child.

"Really? I didn't know they had a bossy-pants section here."

"Actually, I preferred the rocket-blaster section. It was right by the sarcastic-tough-guy section, making it easy to shoot at targets." But her smile caused him to chuckle, and seconds later, she joined him. He liked the sound of her laughter. It was sweet but throaty at the same time. A complete contradiction in terms, much like the woman herself.

"C'mon, partner," he said, placing a hand above the curve of her hip and guiding her toward the Lego area. "According to my calculations, we've got less than nine minutes to accomplish this mission."

Her face turned to his in surprise, but she didn't make an effort to remove his hand or to step away from him.

"Besides," he added. "The manager here knows me by name, and even without the twins with us to wreak havoc, he'll probably still be watching me like a hawk."

"So it's not just Mrs. Duncan who doesn't appreciate your family's patronage in their stores?" She held her body rigid yet shot him a teasing smile. Even though the polished floor was smooth, Luke lost his footing and almost stumbled, causing him to pull her in closer to him.

"I know it's hard to imagine," he said, trying to resume his pace. "But not everyone is as charmed by the Gregson twins as you are."

Carmen stopped and put her hand on his shoulder. Since he had yet to pull his own arm away from her waist, they were standing face-to-face in somewhat of an embrace.

"Luke, your boys are wonderful and you're so lucky to have them. Don't let anyone else's misguided judgments make you think otherwise. Sure, they're a handful and they have a lot of energy. But they also have a lot of compassion. They're smart and sweet and extremely happy. That means you're doing something right."

His throat threatened to close and he sucked in a deep breath, not wanting to get emotional in the walkway between the Matchbox cars and the Nerf guns.

"Thank you for saying that," he said. Then he lifted his eyes to the ceiling and away from her gentle and caring gaze before speaking again. "When their mom died, I felt like I wasn't worthy of being a dad to them. I was gone a lot on deployment, both before and especially after. Some people thought I was running from my responsibilities when I would leave them with my family and go out on dangerous assignments. But I figured it would benefit them more to be raised by people who knew what they were doing. I'd already let Samantha down and I didn't want to let the boys down by not being the father they deserved. It took a…"

The front of Luke's jeans suddenly vibrated, causing Carmen to quickly jump back. He hadn't realized they'd been standing close enough for her to feel it. He fumbled in his pocket before pulling his cell phone out.

Seeing the school's number on the display brought a familiar moment of panic to his chest and he cleared his throat before answering, expecting the worst. Again.

"Hi, Dad." The voice on the other end sounded perfectly healthy and not the least bit in trouble.

"Hi, Aiden," Luke said, noting the worried look in Carmen's eyes. "Is anything wrong?"

"No. We just told the school secretary that you didn't pack us our lunch and she let us call you."

"Hi, Dad," Caden yelled in the background.

"But I gave you both money to eat at the cafeteria today," Luke said, and then mouthed to Carmen that everything was okay.

"I know," Aiden said. "Which means we didn't really tell a lie because technically you didn't pack us one."

"Well, *technically*, you better have a good reason for calling me during school time."

"We do. Are you still shopping with Officer Carmen for our party?" Aiden asked, having apparently overheard Luke's conversation with Kylie last night.

"Yes, I am, but I doubt we're going to have enough time to buy you two any presents if you keep interrupting us."

"Well, Hunter said Mrs. Cooper was inviting us over for dinner tonight because the poker game got canceled. So we just wanted to let you know that you don't need to be back until dinnertime…"

Luke heard some mumbling on the other end of the line before Caden's voice replaced his brother's. "What Aiden meant was that there might not be enough dinner for you guys. So you and Officer Carmen should just stay in Boise and have dinner by yourselves…"

There was more mumbling followed by a scuffling sound, which probably meant Aiden had snatched the receiver back. "Anyway, Mrs. Cooper is gonna pick us up after school so you guys can take your time buying us presents and getting the rest of the stuff for our party. Especially the buying-us-presents part."

"Yeah," Caden's voice called out. "Don't forget that I want the rebel ice fortress. And Aiden wants the pink dream palace! Hey, here comes Nurse Dunn."

"We gotta go, Dad. Tell Officer Carmen hi."

"Bye, you two. Get back to class." Luke disconnected the call.

"What was that all about?" Carmen asked.

He hesitated to tell her because he knew that his children shouldn't be calling him in the middle of the day from school for no good reason. Luke was used to their random antics and didn't want Carmen to read anything into it.

He explained that the boys were going over to Maxine and Cooper's after school, so they could take their time shopping. "Which is a good thing," he said as they stepped into the Lego aisle. "My wallet doesn't want me going grocery shopping on an empty stomach. Let's finish up here and go grab some lunch."

"Lunch, huh?" She grinned again. "We've got a million things to get done today and all you can think about is your stomach?"

"I'm a man. What else am I supposed to think about?"

Certainly, he wasn't supposed to be thinking about how he was going to have Carmen all to himself for the rest of the afternoon.

Chapter Seven

Carmen used the excuse that she was concerned Luke's wallet couldn't handle much more withdrawals today. But the real reason she'd suggested they drive through and pick up fast food was because she didn't think she could handle sitting across the table from him at lunch. Even the strongest of women knew their limitations.

Hey, maybe Abuela should add that to her list of quotes.

Even if Carmen tried to tell herself that going out to eat with Luke was no different than grabbing a sandwich with Cooper on break, or having breakfast with Scooter and Jonesy at the Cowgirl Up Café, Carmen knew her heart shouldn't be tested.

It was tempting enough to pretend that this little shopping trip was like a quasi date, but as soon as she let her mind meander in that direction, it would be too difficult to reverse course. She and Luke were barely friends. More like acquaintances.

"Plus," she argued her point as he steered the Nanamobile out of the Toy Town parking lot, "even with the twins being picked up from school, we still should try and get back to Sugar Falls as soon as we can. Maxine and Cooper are familiar with how long it takes to drive into Boise and stop at a few stores. If we don't get back by dinner, they're going to think something's up."

"Like we got lost or something?" he asked, draping one arm along the back of the plush bench seat as he pulled into traffic.

Her eyes darted back at his hand resting mere inches from her shoulder. "I was thinking more like you and I were up to..." She pinched her lips together and raised her eyebrows, but he was checking out the review mirror instead of her.

"What could we possibly be up to?" He made a smooth right turn at the intersection and Carmen had to wonder how much practice Luke Gregson had at driving one-handed with a female in his passenger seat.

Did she really have to spell it out for him? "That maybe we're enjoying spending time together. You know, *without* the kids."

"Well, why wouldn't we? I mean, I love those little monkeys, but unless I'm at work, I don't get a lot of one-on-one time alone with other adults."

"But this is kind of different than just playing poker with the guys on Thursday nights." She looked back at his relaxed hand again.

His eyes followed hers and he pulled his arm away

so quickly the sudden movement caused him to swerve into the next lane. Another driver blasted their horn and Luke lifted his fingers out the window in an apologetic wave.

"What? Nah. I don't think anyone would think that," he said, then coughed. "But if you'd prefer to grab something to go, there's a Sonic burger place up ahead."

If he was using a burger joint as an attempt to divert her attention away from the subject of them being romantically involved, then maybe he wasn't as smooth as she'd first suspected. Or maybe he wasn't diverting anything. Maybe it was simply too ridiculous for him to contemplate the possibility that other people might think they were on a secret date.

But she'd already put the suggestion out there and now she was kicking herself for bringing it up, since he was clearly not of the same mind-set. How did they go back to normal—or at least, normal for them—after that?

"Burgers sound good," she said, leaning her body closer to the door. She wanted to put as much distance between herself and the awkwardness she'd just created.

Luke chose one of the larger parking spots behind the restaurant and maneuvered the car much too close to the menu sign before asking her what she wanted to eat. Because of his huge, muscular, perfect manly body, she had to lean forward to see around him, bringing her into closer contact. The smell of his aftershave was tickling her nose, tickling her nerves, tickling her ability to think rationally altogether. So she just ordered the first item on the menu that she could read. "I'll take the Coney dog combo with the cheese tots."

"What do you want to drink?" he asked.

Crap. She had to lean forward again and when she did so, he chose that particular second to look her way. His eyes drifted toward the V in her top and she whipped back against the seat quickly. "Cherry lime-ade," she said louder than she intended.

Luke ordered but didn't look at her again, even after the carhop skated out to deliver their food to them. He handed Carmen the bright red drink and she tried to delicately take the foam cup from his hand without touching his fingers. They might as well be tiptoeing around a crime scene; they were both determined to avoid contact with each other.

So maybe he *was* worried that someone else—particularly she—might think their excursion into Boise was a date.

Carmen had done the whole avoidance song and dance with Mark after her surgery and found that it was just better to be direct, cut to the chase and pull the pin out of the conversational grenade once and for all. Then run for cover.

"You know what, Luke," she finally said. "Let's just pretend I never said anything about people getting the wrong idea about us. Obviously neither one of us thinks of this as a date or anything. Besides, even if we *were* attracted to each other, it's not like anything could ever come of it. We're not even friends. So let's just agree that we're both here for the kids' sake and try to work together to make sure their birthday party goes well."

"That's fine," he said, pulling her chili dog out of the paper sack, then holding it out of reach as she tried to take it. "Except for one part. I really do want to be friends, Delgado. You're an important part of Aiden's and Caden's lives and I think it's kind of weird that we can't act more friendly around each other."

She didn't appreciate him holding her lunch hostage, but she did agree with what he was saying. "Fair enough. Friends?"

She held out her hand and he shook it before turning over the chili dog, replacing his warmth with the wrapped gooey mess she'd mistakenly ordered.

"Now that that's settled," she said, "next stop, Costco."

"Actually," he said, snapping open a plastic container, "I can't drive and eat my food."

"What is that? Who orders a chicken salad from a burger joint?"

"The guy who normally lives on a steady diet of Honey Smacks for breakfast and macaroni-based casseroles for dinner. Unless I take the time to cook multiple meals, lunch is the only healthy time of the day for me." He took his time ripping open his ranch dressing, and his tan fingers made an elaborate work out of stroking and squeezing every last drop from the packet. She was too mesmerized to look away. "But now that we decided we're just friends, and that there's nothing more going on, you're not still in a hurry, are you?"

"No," she said, settling back with her cherry limeade. "I'm in no hurry." The only thing she was in was a heap of trouble if she kept looking at him.

Yuck. She hated these sweet artificially flavored drinks, but she'd panicked and ordered the first thing she could think of. But after taking the initiative to confront him on their awkwardness and her attempt to make things seem more normal, she wasn't going to admit she'd much rather be eating the salad, as well.

"Speaking of food," he said, after finishing a few bites. "What exactly does my sister-in-law have planned for the birthday dinner?"

Carmen licked some cheese sauce off her finger before consulting the list. "It looks like grilled chicken, hot dogs, potato salad, baked beans, spinach salad, fresh fruit, that kind of thing."

"That kind of thing? You make it sound so easy."

"You have a grill, don't you?"

"Yeah. The hot dogs are no problem and the chicken might be doable if we buy enough barbecue sauce to cover up the fact that I tend to overcook meat. But I've never made a potato salad or any of that other stuff before."

"That's why I'm here to help you." Carmen almost called him *friend* but didn't want to patronize him or remind him of the reason for their newly formed relationship.

"Do you know how to cook?" He was lifting an eyebrow at her and she wanted to throw a tater tot at him for doubting her.

"Of course I know how to cook."

"Well, it's just that you never really struck me as that type of woman." Was he making another crack about her just being one of the guys? Before she could respond, he added, "You always seem like you'd be way more comfortable on the shooting range than in the kitchen. But then again, after seeing all those froufrou beauty products in your bathroom, maybe I should've known better."

"Whose products are you calling froufrou?" She

threw a tater tot at him, then laughed when he caught it in his mouth.

"Okay, soldier," he said, shoving his empty salad container into the paper bag. "Break's over. Time to get back to work."

She wadded up her napkin and added her half-eaten lunch to the bag before getting out and throwing it all away in the trash bin two spots down from theirs. When she got back in the car, she saw that he'd maneuvered the drinks in the cardboard holder so that his diet soda was now on her side.

He must've detected her observation because he put the car in Drive, then commented, "I needed a taste of something sweet, so I switched them. Besides, you weren't going to drink yours, anyway."

He was right, but she hated the fact that he'd noticed. She also hated the fact that no matter how quickly he'd been willing to agree to their truce, she was dying to give him a taste of something sweet.

They were halfway through Costco and Luke was still replaying her words in his mind.

It's not like anything could ever come of it.

So was she admitting to a mutual attraction between them? Because it kind of sounded like she was. Not that he could be sure. Despite Samantha's accusations to the contrary, Luke was no expert on women or whether they wanted him. Sure, some of his buddies from his former SEAL team used to tease him about his pretty-boy looks, but he'd never been all that interested in what women were thinking when they looked at him.

He only knew that he wasn't capable of giving them what they wanted.

"Do you want breasts or thighs?" he heard her ask, and he almost crashed the shopping cart into the refrigerator case.

"What?" he asked, trying to keep his eyes focused straight ahead so they wouldn't stray below her neck again. As much as he'd appreciated the view when she'd leaned over him to order off the lunch menu, they were in a public place now and his blood pressure didn't need to be spiking like a launched projectile missile.

She lifted the chicken packages higher and repeated her question. "Oh. Both," he said, wishing he could make an inappropriate joke. But she'd made it clear that flirtatious teasing wasn't even an option. Hadn't she?

He clenched his jaw as he pushed the oversize cart down the wide aisles, following her as she added items to it and then made notes on that damn list of Kylie's. He could read GPS coordinates in the dark, but he sure as hell couldn't read the sexy brunette who was walking through the warehouse store like a rear admiral inspecting her crew.

If he didn't have Carmen's perfectly curved butt as the charming view in front of him, Luke would've been tempted to call his sister-in-law and tell her to forget her stupid list. He could just order a bunch of pizzas from Patrelli's instead.

But no matter what Carmen had said earlier, the fact of the matter was he *did* enjoy spending time with her. Especially when she wasn't in her tough-cop mode.

She stopped by a sample display and took a tiny paper cup filled with part of a beef chimichanga, handing it to him before snagging one for herself and taking a bite. "They're not as good as Abuela's, but not too bad for frozen."

"*Abuela* means grandma in Spanish, right?" he asked.

"Yes. She's my dad's mom and the best cook I know. It drives my mom crazy that any time we had a family party, everyone would always ask Abuela to make most of the food. Luckily for you, I emailed her and asked for her potato salad recipe."

"You said *had*." He took the empty sample cup from her and tossed it in the trash.

"Had what?" She must not have noticed the telling slip.

"Any time you *had* a family party. Does that mean you don't have family parties anymore?"

She shrugged, then grabbed a fifty-count package of hot dogs from the case. "I'm sure they still have them. I just haven't attended one in a long time."

"Why not?"

"Because most of my family lives in Las Vegas and I'm up here."

"Don't you miss them?"

"Sure. Sometimes." She tugged on the front end of the cart, but he wasn't going to follow along any more. She'd said they were friends and, as friends, he wanted to learn more about her. He stood still, keeping the cart locked in place until she looked back at him.

"Fine," she said. "I should probably go visit more often but things are kind of awkward right now. Besides, it's not like my family isn't used to the distance.

I joined the Marine Corps straight out of high school and was stationed all over, including two deployments to the Middle East."

He nodded. "I get that. My own parents live in Boise, and after Drew and I joined up, we all just got accustomed to going for long periods without seeing each other."

"So there you have it," she said, then walked around the corner to the next aisle without waiting for him to follow.

"But here's what I don't understand," he said, catching up to her. Man, this cart was getting heavier to push by the minute. "You moved back to Vegas after you got out of the military and you became a police officer there, right?"

"Right…" Her tense shoulders suggested she wanted to roll her eyes, but instead she kept her head down, staring at the list. He was getting closer to uncovering something. He could feel it.

"Now, I'm just speaking from personal experience, so bear with me. But now that I've moved back to Idaho to be close to my family and my hometown, I can't imagine ever packing up and leaving again."

"Is there supposed to be a question in there?"

Whoa. She'd gone from annoyed to defensive in a snap. *Reel it back in, Gregson.* Luke shifted from one foot to the other.

"Listen." He shot her a grin and tried to make his voice sound more teasing. "Not all of us can be trained cops and interrogators. Anyway, you said things were awkward with your family now. Plus, out of the blue you recently moved to some nowhere town in Idaho to take a job on a tiny police force even though you don't know anyone in Sugar Falls. So I'm just wondering if those things go hand in hand."

"You're wrong about the part that I didn't know anyone in Sugar Falls. I was stationed at Camp Lejeune with Cooper, and when he said he was building up a new department out here it seemed like a good time to change course. But there *is* one thing you're right about. You're not a trained interrogator."

She'd felt the need to change course. He'd keep that little nugget of information stored for future use.

"So train me," he said, moving next to her so he could help her load cases of soda. They were going to need a forklift soon. "If you wanted to know all about someone's past, how would you go about asking them?"

"Well, I wouldn't do it in the beverage aisle of Costco." Her controlled smile was appealing and gave a hint of sauciness. But Luke wasn't satisfied yet.

"Should I have asked once we got to the checkout line?" he asked, deciding to banter with her while he bided his time.

"Nah. If it were me, I'd wait until my subject was frustrated with the impossible task of cramming all these groceries into the trunk of the Nanamobile and then spring my questions on them when they were too overwhelmed and distracted to gauge their answers."

"Fine," he said, taking a cup of green juice from the next sampling station and handing it to her. "I'll hold all my personal questions until then. I knew there was a good reason for bringing my car."

There went her pretty blush again. And, despite the shot of organic kale smoothie he'd just swallowed, his mouth went dry.

"Hmm," she said, and smirked. "Maybe the question you should be asking is how many ice chests are you going to need to borrow to hold all these drinks? We haven't even gotten to the beer section yet."

He laughed, not so much at her attempt to scare him back into birthday-party-planning action, but at her feeble attempt to thwart his curiosity. Her refusal to talk about this only made him more determined to breach her heavily guarded walls.

Apparently Officer Delgado didn't realize that once a SEAL took on a mission, he didn't give up until he got the job done.

Sure enough, the blasted man took Carmen's tongue-in-cheek advice to heart and decided that the best time to bring up her family history was while she was trying to figure out how to shove the hot dog buns into his trunk without risking the bag of potatoes crushing against them the moment he made the turn onto the highway back toward Sugar Falls.

"Luke, I wasn't serious about you interrogating me out here in the parking lot."

"Hey, if you're going to be calling me Luke all the time, I'm making the executive decision that it's only fair if I call you Carmen."

She didn't want to point out that he'd already called her that before, and that when he did her heart expanded and her resistance began slipping. So, instead, she blew a stray curl out of her eyes and tried to be as nonchalant as possible. "I don't care what you call me."

There. That sounded believable.

"I think some of this stuff is going to have to be squished up front with us," he said when it became obvious there was nowhere else to put the huge bags of chips and the new plastic oars she'd decided to buy the boys. After all, they'd recovered the canoe, but their paddles had been washed away when they'd lost control of their craft in the river behind her house about a month ago.

But the extra stuff in front was just fine with her. Maybe the additional barrier between them would prevent him from asking any more questions.

Nope, she realized as soon as they turned onto the highway and he said, "Okay, we have an hour back to Sugar Falls. That should be plenty of time to tell me about why things are awkward in your family."

"Oh, come on, Luke. You don't really want to know all this, do you? Hey, listen." She turned up Blake Shelton's voice on the radio. "This is one of my favorite songs."

"No way, *Carmen*." He reached over and switched the knob into the off position. Maybe they should've stuck to using last names. "I need to know what kind of person is going to be making the potato salad for my party tomorrow."

"The kind of person who can pass multiple departmental background checks, as well the person who you entrust your children to every Tuesday afternoon for the Sugar Falls Elementary mentorship program."

"Background checks and fingerprints are all fine and good, but I take my side dishes seriously. So spill it."

"Fine." She leaned her head against the velvet upholstered headrest and looked at the sun sinking lower, just like her resolve. "What do you want to know?"

"Why did you leave Vegas PD?"

"I wanted a change of pace."

"That's a vague answer."

"It's the only one I'm willing to give."

"So then when's the last time you saw your family?"

"About nine months ago. My dad and brothers helped me move into the cottage where I live now."

"So you haven't been back to visit since you relocated to Sugar Falls?"

"No." But before he could fire off another question, she said, "My turn to ask something."

"Shoot," he said. "My life's an open book." She took that as an implication that hers wasn't.

"When I saw the scar on your rib cage, you said that the tattoo was the date you became a father. But it's different than the date the twins were born."

"Is there a question in there somewhere?" he asked, throwing her own line back at her.

"What's the significance of that?" she continued.

"The significance is that after the boys' mom died, I spent a lot of time running from my responsibilities. Hell, Samantha would say that I was running from them way before she died. But, like I said earlier today, I thought the twins were better off without me as their primary caregiver."

"Why would they be better off without you?"

"Uh-uh, Officer. My turn. Why haven't you been to Las Vegas since you moved here? You said you come from a large family and you're used to large parties. I find it hard to believe that they haven't had some sort of big celebration since you left. And your hometown isn't all that far. So why haven't you been back?"

"Because the last big family celebration was my

cousin Maria Rosa's wedding and I didn't feel like going. Why would the twins be better off without you?"

"Actually, this back-and-forth questioning is too confusing," Luke said. "I'll make you a deal. Five questions at a time. Let me get to the bottom of this one thing, and then you can ask me whatever else you want."

Carmen didn't think that was particularly fair, but the man had a point. It was getting tricky to keep track of whose personal story they were following and she wanted him focused if she hoped to get real answers out of him about his relationship with his kids. And, if she were honest with herself, about his late wife. "All right. Go ahead."

"Why wouldn't you want to go to your own cousin's wedding?"

She stole a glance at Luke over the five-pound bag of Ruffles, but he was keeping his eyes on the highway. Everyone in her family knew, but nobody actually brought it up to her—probably to protect her feelings. This would be the first time she'd said it out loud or talked about it to anyone, so at least he wasn't looking at her.

She took a calm breath and then forced the words out. "Because she was marrying my ex-boyfriend."

Carmen had to give Luke credit for not completely skidding off the road when she'd made that announcement. Instead, he'd only swerved a little and then overcorrected his steering, causing the rear tires to fishtail briefly before straightening out.

"Did you just say that your cousin married your ex-boyfriend?"

"Yep."

"Did she know he was your ex?"

"Yep."

"Did this jerk know she was your cousin?"

"Mark isn't really a jerk," she admitted. Just a man who wanted what Carmen couldn't give him.

"How can you defend him?"

"Well, I didn't say I was *happy* about the wedding. I just said he wasn't a jerk. I was the one who broke things off with him." More like she'd been the one to let him off the hook and he'd eagerly jumped at the chance. Either way, Carmen was the one responsible for it all. Putting herself at risk was one of the downfalls to having a dangerous job.

"But still," he said. She couldn't see his expression, but his tone was incredulous. "Your own cousin? There wasn't anyone else he could've married?"

"My Tia Lupe offered, but she's seventy-eight, so my cousin was probably the better match."

"You seem so calm and unaffected by the whole situation," he said.

Unaffected? Hardly. Yet, what could she do but try to remain calm? And try to justify her reality as something completely ordinary.

"You know how I mentioned that my big family loves to get together for dinners?" she asked, but didn't wait for his response. "Well, Mark attended plenty of those dinners and got to know all of them pretty well."

"But you'd think that once you broke up with the jerk—I mean the *guy*, and I use that term loosely—their loyalty would stick with you."

"Well, now their loyalty is with Maria Rosa. Besides, my family all understood why we broke up and nobody could really blame Mark."

"So they blamed you? I don't get it. What'd you do

that was so bad you deserved to have your ex run off and marry your cousin?"

Carmen shook her head, not wanting to admit to him or anyone the responsibility she felt for her injury—for her wounds that would never heal. But, with the sun sinking behind the mountain, she doubted he could see her in the darkened interior of the car. Plus, if he didn't keep his eyes on the road, he would miss the turn for his cabin. But he skillfully maneuvered the bulky Oldsmobile over the ruts along his dirt driveway while curiously glancing her way, which meant that she needed to get herself in check right now. She ran a hand through her curly hair, wishing she could reach a ponytail holder in her purse and pull it under control, pull herself under control.

"Unfortunately, your five questions are up, Captain Gregson." She tried to make her voice sound cheery. "And we need to get this car unloaded before the ice cream melts all over the cheese tray."

Chapter Eight

Luckily for her, Luke couldn't do much talking as they carried in load after load of party supplies and groceries.

"We should've picked up something to eat on the way home," he said after Carmen finished transferring several items to her own car so she could prepare some of the side dishes at home. "That salad didn't last long and I'm starved."

"Luke, you have so much food in your fridge, we could barely get it closed. I'm sure you can find something."

"Yeah, but the only thing already made is the hummus and the veggie tray." He looked at his watch. "Hey, maybe if we hurry, we can make it to Cooper and Maxine's before they put dinner away."

Not a chance. There was no way Carmen was going

to show up at his friend's house with him for a family meal. That was just way too…couple-like.

"You go on ahead," she said. "I'm going to take some of this stuff to my house and get a head start on the cooking tonight."

"Hmm, maybe I should just come over to your house and test out the menu before I serve it to my guests."

"*Your* guests? You mean the hundred and fifty or so people you had no idea were coming tomorrow?"

"Yeah." He revealed that dimple and the butterfly wings inside her started flapping again. "Those."

"It'll take too long. I think you may have better luck at Cooper and Maxine's. Besides, the kids are probably waiting for you."

"You're right," he said, the divot in his cheek disappearing. Was he disappointed she wasn't inviting him over for uncooked potato salad?

"Oh, before I forget," he said, the dimple returning. "I have something for you."

He ran into his bedroom and she tried not to let her imagination run right back there with him. Luckily, he returned a second later and she no longer had to force herself to not contemplate following him.

"Here." He threw a wadded-up ball of blue fabric at her.

"What's this?" She held it up.

"I figured I owed you a T-shirt since I ripped yours the other week."

She looked at the white vinyl USN logo and the words below that read Tough Girls Wear Anchors and then burst into laughter.

"I like seeing you laugh, Carmen." If he liked that,

then he'd probably love seeing the way her heart danced around inside her chest whenever he smiled at her.

"Thanks for giving me a reason to." She'd needed it. Especially after such an unlaughable conversation in the car. "And don't forget to wrap those presents before you pick up the twins. You know they're going to be a couple of live wires tonight and all kinds of excited for their party tomorrow."

"They're a couple of live wires even when they *don't* have a birthday party to look forward to."

She smiled again, finding the urge more natural the longer she stood in front of him.

"And thanks for all your help shopping," he said. Was it her imagination or was he closer? "You really didn't have to do all that."

"Really, Luke, it was no problem. I was off anyway today and I can be here first thing tomorrow to help with the rest of the setup."

Yep, he was definitely moving in closer to her. Maybe he was just in a hurry to get out the door and was trying to maneuver her into leaving.

She made a move to grab her purse off the small entry table just as he was reaching for his keys. At least, she *thought* he'd been reaching for his keys. But the moment their fingers brushed, it felt so natural, as though it was what they'd both been intending all along.

His hand clamped down over hers, leaving her purse and all her good judgment out of reach. His grip was firm but not forceful. She was a martial arts expert and could break his hold if she really wanted to. But at this exact second, she didn't.

"I have just one more question, Carmen." Her name on his lips was its own sentence. Its own question.

And her answer was yes. Hell, yes. But she couldn't let him see that. So she held herself perfectly still, her eyes under strict orders from her brain to not meet his. If her pupils went AWOL, then she was in big trouble.

"Since you broke up with that Mark guy who isn't a jerk, do you have any current jerk boyfriends that I should know about?"

Her heartbeat was throbbing so loudly in her ears she wondered if she'd misheard the question. When she didn't answer, Luke used his free hand to lift her chin up so her traitorous eyes were forced to look directly into his. "What do you mean?"

"I was asking if you currently have a boyfriend."

"No." She barely managed to breathe out the word.

"Good. Then nobody will mind when I do this." Luke kept his grip on her hand as he wrapped his arm around her waist, using her own limb as a willing accomplice in anchoring her body to his. The tilt of his head left no question as to what he was going to do next.

After securing her against his body, Luke lowered his lips to hers. He'd already been waiting too damn long to kiss her. And oh, man, were her full, sweet lips worth the wait.

Carmen's fingers twined with his and squeezed his hand. But judging by the fervent pressure of her mouth, she had no intention of backing away.

He angled her jaw so that he could deepen the kiss, but as soon as he opened his lips to begin his assault, her tongue made the first move. She delved deeply inside his mouth, exploring him before he could do the same to her.

He felt her free arm sweep against his shoulder before curving along the back of his neck as she rose up on her toes to meet him. Her cool fingers dipped below the cotton neckline of his shirt and he returned the gesture by skimming his own hand along the waistband of her jeans. He released her other arm and she quickly brought it up and wrapped herself around him, the movement lifting the edge of her sweater and allowing him a strip of access to the smooth, warm skin below.

She made a little mewling sound, which allowed him the chance to overpower her tongue and gain entrance to plunder her depths, to make the same explorations she'd already made. His hands splayed wider, resting just under her rib cage, and he wished he could touch all of her at once.

He wanted to move his hands toward her breasts, to feel the taut nipples that had teased him so badly that day at her house. But her body was pressed up so close against his own he couldn't bring himself to move away from her long enough to do so.

Instead, he slid his hands lower, cupping her bottom as he pulled her against his erection. Her hips moved slightly, as though she was seeking to fit herself over him, and he groaned, moving his lips along her jawline and down her neck.

He wanted to taste more of her. But before he could make it to her collarbone, he heard a musical-like wailing sound in the distance. Carmen took a step back and, though she seemed to be panting just as deeply as he was, she moved to open the door.

"It's just another ice-cream truck," he said, reaching for her waist to pull her back.

"No." She shook her head, as though she could shake off the passion they'd just shared. "That's a police siren. Luke, I've got to go."

"I thought you were off duty today."

"I'm never off duty," she said, grabbing her purse and jogging toward her SUV, still parked in the driveway. Her cell phone was at her ear before she'd even started the engine.

He had to lean on the doorjamb to prop his still-reeling body up, his feet feeling wobbly as they tried to arch over the uneven threshold. At least, he told himself it was because of where he was standing. He wasn't ready to admit that their kiss had practically knocked his legs out from under him.

And judging by her response, she'd been just as affected as him. He'd tried to relax and let her lead in the kiss, but there was something about the normally in-control Carmen Delgado that made Luke want to be in charge. It was probably his sense that he had absolutely no control when it came to her.

Of course, she'd apparently been able to shake it off better—literally—and spring right back into tough-cop mode.

As he watched her taillights disappear down his driveway, he had a flashback to a time when the boys were still crawling. Samantha was taking a video of them on her phone when Luke got a call from his commander and had rushed out of their Coronado apartment.

I'm never off duty.

He'd said those exact same words to Samantha,

who'd yelled back that, just once, he should think about his duty to his family. It had taken a family disaster and a near-death experience, but that duty was now clearer than ever. Just as his desire for Officer Maria Carmen Delgado was now clearer than ever.

Luke stood there in his doorway feeling a lot less guilty than he probably had a right to be. Carmen's abrupt departure was a reminder of all the times he'd done the exact same thing for the exact same reason. He couldn't say he was experiencing a feeling of empathy, because, unlike his wife, he didn't resent Carmen's dangerous job. In fact, a small part of him—that impulsive part he tried to keep locked away—was actually envious of it. That was enough to add to his already burdened complex about all the mistakes he'd made in the past.

Yet, as ashamed as he was to admit it, none of his guilt was because he'd just kissed another woman and felt more grounded than he ever had.

Luke was standing in front of the borrowed grill, a cold bottle of Samuel Adams in his hand, as he talked to his twin brother, Drew.

"You remember any of our birthday parties being this big?" Drew asked.

Luke looked around at all the Sugar Falls residents who had come to celebrate his children turning nine. His yard was a madhouse, but at least with Kylie and Carmen running things, it had the appearance of controlled chaos.

"Nope." Luke shook his head. "Not even the party we had in fourth grade where Mrs. Giddles told us we had to invite everyone in our class. Including the girls."

"That's right. I seem to recall Mom and Dad throwing in the towel after that one. Every year after that, we got to pick one friend to bring with us to play miniature golf."

"Our parents were saints."

"Still are," Drew said before taking a sip of his own beer. "Too bad they couldn't make it today."

Donna and Jerry Gregson were enjoying their well-earned retirement, crisscrossing the United States in their Fleetwood Bounder. "Mom called the other day," Luke said. "I told her about the boys making the Little League all-star team and their first tournament in Rexburg. They said they'll try and make it back in time for that."

"Good. Maybe Kylie and I will make the trip with the girls. It'll give the folks a chance to see all their grandchildren at once."

Luke flipped over the chicken. "Speaking of parents, the boys seem to be adjusting pretty well to having just me around."

"They really have," his brother agreed. And Drew should know. He and Kylie had kept the twins for part of the summer when Luke had been on that last life-changing mission. "I know Kylie wishes she could spend more time with them. Maybe once we get the girls on a better sleep schedule, we can plan to have them over for a night."

"That would be nice. You know I worry about them not having a mother figure in their life."

Drew squeezed his shoulder. "I know. But they have you and you shouldn't be selling yourself short."

"Carmen has been spending a lot of time with them, and that seems to help." Luke felt like he was testing the temperature of something other than the meat on the grill.

"Carmen's great," Drew agreed. "Kylie told me she really helped you pull off this party."

"Party? More like a three-ring circus. But I think Kylie was well aware of what she was doing."

Luke was adding hot dogs to the upper rack and didn't see the quick look of culpability flash across Drew's face. "What do you mean?"

"I mean, your wife rented all these tables and bounce houses and hired that goofy guy in the superhero costume without even telling me because she knew I'd say no. And don't even get me started on that petting zoo in the driveway so that the younger kids would have something to do, too."

Drew let out a breath and Luke, knowing his twin, immediately picked up on his normally relaxed brother's release of tension. Why should he be relieved? Did he think Luke was actually annoyed with his sweet but over-the-top wife?

"Don't get me wrong," Luke defended. "I really do appreciate all her work and how much she loves the boys. I was just saying it was a godsend that she talked Carmen into pinch-hitting for her because I wouldn't have been able to pull this off by myself."

"It's Carmen now, huh?"

"Well, we spent the whole day together yesterday and it's kind of hard not to become friends when you're debating what kind of candy to stuff in the piñatas and how many sets of plastic silverware to buy."

"So you're *just* friends?" Drew arched one golden eyebrow above the rim of his wire-framed glasses.

Dammit. Luke should've known that his psychologist twin knew him better than that. Of course, wasn't that exactly what he'd been counting on when he'd brought up this conversation in the first place? He needed to talk to someone about what had happened between him and the woman who'd set his body into high alert before racing away from his house last night in hot pursuit of justice.

"Okay, here's the deal," Luke said, then leaned in toward his brother. "I sort of…kissed her."

"You *what*?"

Quickly, Luke confided a few of the details that had taken place less than twenty-four hours ago. He kept his voice low, because even though all the other adults seemed to be either gorging themselves on onion dip or chasing the children around the makeshift laser tag zone, this was a small town and he didn't want anyone overhearing him.

"So how'd you feel afterward?" Drew asked when Luke finished speaking.

"How do you think I felt?"

"Not physically, moron. I mean emotionally."

"I felt fine. I guess."

"Come on, Luke. You can do better than that. You have a shrink for a brother. If you want me to psychoanalyze this relationship, you need to give me more than that to go on."

"Who says I want you to psychoanalyze anything, Dr. Annoying?" Luke looked up just in time to see Carmen refilling a huge bowl of chips on one of the food tables. "And who says we're in a relationship?"

A small fire leaped up between the grate and Drew shoved him aside, taking the barbecue tongs from him. "Here, hotshot. Let me get things under control for you. As usual." His brother was used to Luke's impulsive nature and his tendency to fly by the seat of his pants. And he was used to bailing Luke out of trouble when the need arose. So it was a habit to stand by and watch his brother quickly move the meat out of the way of the flames, waiting for Drew to help him make sense of the scorching situation he'd caused last night when he'd kissed Carmen.

"I hate to point out the obvious, Luke," his twin finally said once the heat of the grill returned to normal. "But you're a single man and, as far as I know, Carmen is a single woman. Why can't you guys enter into a mature, consenting relationship like two normal adults?"

"But what about my kids?"

"What about them? I thought it was pretty common knowledge that they're crazy about Carmen and they like having her around."

"Sure they do. But what about when I can't be the kind of man Carmen deserves and we inevitably break up? The twins would be devastated."

"Listen, Luke. I bit my tongue for almost six years because I knew you needed time to grieve for your wife and come to terms with your perceived guilt over her death."

"My guilt isn't perceived." He crossed his arms over his chest and kicked at a pinecone near his foot. "It's very real and very justified. I was never the kind of husband Samantha deserved. I don't want to make that mistake again."

"What do you mean you weren't the kind of husband she deserved? You were you, Luke."

"What kind of psychobabble is that?" Luke asked, then made the mistake of watching Carmen grab an open bottle of wine from the temporary bar set up near the back porch. He really wanted to ask Kylie who had a bar at a children's birthday party, but frankly he needed another beer himself. Besides, if they were going to have a mobile petting zoo, they might as well have some booze to keep all the parents more relaxed.

"It means that you did the best you could," Drew said gently. "Samantha knew you were a SEAL when she met you at that bar in Coronado. She knew you were a SEAL when she got pregnant with the twins and you talked her into marrying you. Anyone who has spent more than five minutes in your company knows where your heart is. You love your boys and you love your family, but up until that point, the Navy and your team were your life. I don't want to speak ill of the dead, but Samantha was well aware of what she was getting into."

"That doesn't mean it was fair that I abandoned her and the boys every time I got called out on an assignment."

"I agree," Drew said. "Being a Navy spouse is a tough life. That's why my department offers classes and workshops and support groups for people in the same position she'd been in. She was fully aware that there was help out there. Hell, I called her once a week to check in and to give her recommendations of places where she could go for assistance. But she chose to deal with your absence and her stress in her own way. It ended up being an unhealthy and fateful way, but that was *her* choice. Luke, being a SEAL did *not* make you a bad husband or a bad father. It made you *you*. When are you going to be done serving your penance for Samantha's death?"

Luke was quiet for a moment. "I don't know. Maybe never. Or maybe I was done last night. Who the hell knows?"

"What do you mean maybe you were done last night?"

"I mean, after I kissed Carmen, I didn't really have any of that guilt I should've felt. It would have been easier if I had."

"So, circling back to my original question, what did you feel after you kissed her?"

"Great," he said. "Happy. Aroused."

"Don't need to hear the last part," his proper brother said, probably wishing his hands were free so he could cover his saintly ears. "What about after she left to go chase bad guys?"

Luke had found out today from Cooper that chasing bad guys actually meant assisting on a call to rescue a group of drunk tourists who'd lost their car in the Snow Creek Lodge parking lot and had no business being behind the wheel, anyway. But he knew that her job was dangerous and someday she might get called out to deal with some pretty dicey situations. He was actually fine with it. No—more than fine. He was pretty impressed.

"I had this weird sense of reverse déjà vu," Luke admitted. "Like I was used to being the one being called out on duty, but now I was experiencing what Samantha must've felt anytime I'd left unexpectedly like that."

"How did you respond to being in that situation for the first time?"

"I didn't respond. How could I? I was proud of Carmen for her dedication to her job and I wasn't about to stand in her way. Maybe a little worried for her, but I wasn't jealous or feeling abandoned. More than anything, I was confused and wanted some reassurance that what had just happened between us wasn't a colossal mistake. But she left without giving me any clue and I can't trust my own instincts when it comes to stuff like this. Then I was too busy thinking about what would happen when I saw her again."

"And now you've seen her again. So how are you feeling about it today?"

"Like I can't wait to kiss her again."

"Then what's stopping you?"

"The fact that she might not want me to. How am I supposed to know what she's thinking?"

"Have you thought about asking her?"

Drew made it sound so simple. Yet, Luke had learned that just because a woman said she was fine with something, didn't mean she was happy about it.

He shrugged. "We haven't had a second alone. She's been pretty good at avoiding me."

Drew grinned. "Well, she isn't avoiding you now. Look alive, brother. She's coming this way."

Chapter Nine

"How much longer do you think the chicken is going to be?" Carmen tried to sound as businesslike as possible when she asked Luke the question.

See. They were just a couple of *friends*. She might argue that today they were coworkers, partnering up together to work on this birthday task force. She'd even responded to his call for backup when Caden had led one of the goats from the petting zoo into the bounce house. "The younger guests are getting restless and their parents need something to soak up all the wine and beer. I was wondering when we should start bringing out some of the side dishes."

She'd been careful to make sure that the only time she'd spoken to him—or gotten within a twelve-foot radius of him—was when there were plenty of witnesses around to stop her from leaping into his arms and picking up right where they'd left off last night. And what better witness than his straight-laced brother, Dr. Gregson, also nicknamed Saint Drew.

"The hot dogs are done now. By the time you get stuff set out, I should have the first batch of chicken ready to go." Luke smiled at her and she searched his expression and his words for any sign of what he was feeling. But he was too used to masking his emotions.

So if he was knee-deep in regret, he'd be extra careful not to give off any sign or show any weakness. Just like her.

"Here, Luke," Drew said, piling the last of the grilled hot dogs onto a tray. "You help Carmen get the food out and I'll bring the chicken over when it's ready. Besides, you should be enjoying the festivities."

Carmen wasn't sure, but she'd thought the doctor had possibly winked at Luke. Her stomach dropped at the implications of what that could mean. Had Luke told his brother what they'd done inside the family cabin last night? That she'd made a fool of herself in his arms, then run off at the first wail of a siren?

Hopefully, Dr. Gregson just had smoke tickling his bespectacled eye, because she would be mortified if anyone from this town suspected she'd been so weak to fall for a couple of harmless kisses. And some arousing caresses. And the feel of his hands on her... Ugh.

She turned to go into the kitchen in order to carry out the bowls and platters of food she'd worked on last night after getting home. The police call she hadn't needed to respond to ended up being a couple of drunk tourists that one of the other officers had easily been able to handle on his own. Her cop instinct had been to rush into the fray. It just so happened that timing wise, her woman-in-over-her-head instinct had been to look for any excuse to get the hell out of Luke's too-intoxicating embrace.

She'd tossed and turned all night thinking about his kiss and the many ways it was going to affect her rapport with the twins once she told Luke that it was best if she didn't spend any more time directly with him. After the way she'd behaved last night, she didn't think she could trust herself around him. A relationship with her was a dead end for any man looking for something permanent. And a man like Luke, who was committed to his family and was hoping for more children, would eventually be relieved in the long run.

By oh two hundred, she'd decided that she'd get through today, focusing on giving Aiden and Caden a memorable birthday party. Then she'd wean herself from their lives. By oh six hundred, she'd given up on any more sleep and had gone into her kitchen to keep herself busy prepping food until it was time to go over to the Gregson cabin.

Luckily, getting the yard decorated and the party set up had kept her and Luke out of each other's way until all the guests arrived. Now she just needed to get through dinner and then she could officially end her shift and save her soul.

Carmen was pulling a pan of baked beans from the oven when she heard the hinges creak on the back screen door. She turned to see Luke standing there in his cargo shorts and polo shirt, looking twice as good as he'd looked last night. Abuela always said, *La fruta prohibida es siempre la mas dulce.* Unfortunately, that woman was usually spot on about recipes and forbidden fruit always being sweeter.

"What can I do to help?" he asked.

"We need to get this and the rest of the side dishes outside." She nodded her head toward the counter loaded down with bowls of potato, macaroni and spinach salads. "Kylie made some sort of coleslaw thing with raisins and marshmallows, but I think she used butter lettuce instead of cabbage so we might want to accidentally forget that in the fridge."

"My sister-in-law isn't exactly known for her skills in the kitchen." Luke grabbed a dish towel and took the hot dish from her hands. She expected him to take it outside, but instead he set it directly down on the kitchen table.

"Actually," she said, not wanting to sound too bossy but needing to get this situation and her battling emotions under control. "I was thinking we should put all the food on the *outside* tables so that people aren't coming in and out of your house."

"I know the food is going outside, Carmen. But right now, I have you *inside*. Alone." Her body, which was in good physical shape for responding to emergency situations, went limp and tense all at once.

"But we need to get people fed," she said, wanting to deter him. When he moved in front of her, she held up her hands as though she could stop him from what she'd secretly been hoping he'd start again.

He looked at the rooster-shaped potholders on her hands before grinning and sliding them off. "Luke," she whispered, even though she doubted anyone else was in the house. "What are you doing?"

"What do you think I'm doing?"

But before his playful lips could get any closer, the back door screeched open. Carmen jumped away from him, backing into the open oven, which was probably less likely to leave a lasting burn than his heated embrace. At least mentally.

"Do you need anything in here?" Kylie said as she walked into the kitchen. "Oh, hey, Luke. I didn't know you were giving Carmen a hand."

He was actually about to give her a lot more than a hand, but Carmen turned to gather the basket full of condiments before the other woman noticed anything was off between the two of them.

"I'd love some help," Carmen said, seizing on the opportunity to put more distance, or at least more obstacles, between her and the man she shouldn't be left alone with. "Luke was just about to start carrying out some of the food, so if you could take a bowl or two outside, that'd be great."

Nobody said a word about the fact that this party and its organization had been Kylie's idea in the first place. After all, this was Kylie's family and, by default, this kitchen should've been her domain. Yet, Luke's sister-in-law seemed willing—actually, eager—to turn over her planning and hostessing role to someone who was a little more than a glorified babysitter.

"Perfect," Kylie said, turning her back to them and opening the refrigerator. "Let me just get my Waldorf coleslaw out of the—oh, no. Why does it look so wilted already?"

Carmen used the distraction to make a fast break toward the back porch.

"We'll finish our conversation later." Luke's whispered words caught Carmen by surprise and she fumbled her grip on the screen door.

She turned to whisper back and her head nearly

collided with Luke's since he was so close behind her. "But we weren't really having a conversation."

"I know." His lips grazed the side of her neck and she almost dropped the ketchup and mustard she'd been balancing in the crook of her arm. She could actually feel the vibration of his laughter against her collarbone. "Here, let me get that for you."

His hand skimmed her waist as he reached in front of her and closed his fingers over hers, helping her release the door latch. A crowd of hungry guests looked up toward them and Carmen walked outside, her legs feeling about as firm as the hot dog buns she was trying to carry in her shaky grip.

"Food's on," Luke announced jovially from behind her.

She deposited the condiments and buns and retreated to the kitchen for more dishes. And maybe that plastic cup of wine she'd poured earlier. She passed Kylie, who was carrying more food and didn't mention the wilted green-and-purple mess Carmen spied dumped into the trash can.

It took several minutes to get her breathing back to normal. By the time the guests had lined up for the buffet-style meal, Alex Russell had taken over on the grill. She wasn't sure where Luke was, but Carmen was glad he was getting a reprieve to enjoy his sons' party since he'd been working so hard on it the past two days.

Freckles, defying both gravity and age, balanced three plates of chicken in one hand as she strutted by wearing bright orange cowboy boots and a halter top to match. "Great party, you two."

You two? Who was…? Carmen felt Luke's palm against her lower back.

"Thanks, Freckles," Luke said, his fingers making a slow small circle before he walked away to tell the children to go wash their hands.

The rest of the evening, Luke made a habit of sneaking up behind Carmen when she was least expecting it, touching her ever so subtly, then taking off seconds later. She prayed that Elaine Marconi, who was holding court near the makeshift bar, hadn't noticed.

But Luke was a master at the hit-and-run displays of affection. A quick caress here, a soft smile there— he'd even refilled her wine cup when she finally took a break to sit and talk with Maxine and Cooper and Mia and Garrett McCormick.

"This is going to be a tough birthday party to top," Maxine said when Luke eventually stayed still long enough to pull out the chair next to Carmen's and take a seat. "I saw one of Mia's dance moms over by the mobile video game trailer asking the face painter if he was available for her daughter's princess party next month.

"You can thank my charming sister-in-law for that," Luke replied, then lifted a cold bottle of beer to his lips. *Stop staring at his lips*, Carmen had to command herself. "I had no idea she was orchestrating all this."

The group of friends all turned to look at the pseudo-carnival that had magically sprung up on Luke's property. He took the opportunity to slide his hand onto Carmen's knee beneath the table.

"Just be thankful my wife told the party-rental people there were only three acres of land here," Drew said. "Do you know that company rents snow-cone booths, inflatable waterslides and human-sized hamster balls?"

Carmen was more thankful that the woman had had the foresight to rent these long green linen tablecloths instead of going with the short plastic ones Luke wanted to buy at the supply store yesterday. Otherwise, everyone would be able to see Luke's hand slowly inching its way up the leg she was praying wouldn't tremble.

"Don't worry, babe," Kylie said to her husband as she fed one of her daughters. "I'm getting plenty of practice for the girls' first birthday."

Drew paled slightly, then recovered and said, "Too bad we don't have the space for all that at our condo. Maybe we'll just have a nice intimate family dinner."

"Don't be silly," Luke chimed in, still not removing his hand from under the table. "This is still Gregson land. You can have the party here. Carmen and I would be happy to help."

Everyone laughed and Carmen tried not to shift in the white plastic folding chair. He made it seem like they were a pair, that they were partners. Even if he'd been sly in the way he'd been touching her all evening, people might already be lumping the two of them together, assuming she would be around for future Gregson family events.

She really needed to get Luke alone to tell him that this birthday party, as well as that kiss last night, was a onetime thing. She needed to convince him that he and the twins were probably better off not getting too close to her. The problem was getting him alone. And then not falling victim to those damn dimples.

* * *

"But, Dad, we don't want to help clean up," Caden told Luke. "Now that everyone's gone, we want to open our presents."

"And have another piece of cake," Aiden whined before shoving a blue lollipop from his piñata treat bag into his mouth.

Luke stood in his almost-empty yard. The party rental company had loaded up and left his property looking like less of a carnival and more an abandoned battlefield. Most of the guests had gone home, with the exception of a few friends who were either collecting remnants of streamers and empty plastic cups or putting his house back to rights.

"See Officer Carmen in the kitchen?" Luke pointed to the window framing her as she washed dishes at the sink and laughed at something one of the other women must've said.

For the first time, Luke realized that his feet hadn't been restless at all today. Sure, they were tired and aching as he'd been standing since seven that morning, but they felt grounded. Seeing Carmen in his home, having her work beside him for a common goal, feeling her eyes on him when she thought no one was looking, felt grounded.

"What about her, Dad?" Aiden interrupted his trailing thoughts.

"Oh, look," Caden yelled before dropping his plastic garbage bag and running toward the driveway. "Uncle Kane's here."

Kane Chatterson pulled up in his old SUV. While the famous baseball pitcher wasn't Luke's brother-in-law exactly, he was Drew's—which made him family and somewhat of an uncle figure to the boys.

The late arrival turned his engine off and grabbed a couple of oversize gift bags from the backseat, causing the boys to shriek and jump up and down over the idea of more presents. Great. At this rate, he'd never get his children to settle down.

Oh, well. They'd probably get more done with the boys out of the way and occupied.

"Good timing." Luke walked up and shook the man's hand. "Did Kylie assign you cleanup duty tonight?"

"Yep. She knows how I feel about avoiding big crowds. Got any beer left?"

"You bet. Come on into the kitchen and we'll get you a plate of food, too. Your sister had me buy enough to feed the crew of an aircraft carrier." What Luke didn't say was thank God Carmen had been there to help him prepare everything, or he'd have been at a complete loss.

Carmen's feet were probably just as tired as his. He thought of the one time he'd seen them bare, her dainty toes with their bright pink polish nervously hustling around on her cottage floor as she brought him and the boys T-shirts to borrow. He would love to send the rest of the cleanup squad home and sit on the sofa with her pretty feet in his lap. He didn't even need her pricey peppermint tree-bark foot cream.

If it were just them, the kids would be in bed and he'd start a fire in the big stone hearth. Maybe put on some of the country music that she enjoyed. His mind started to get lost in the fantasy, but was cut short when he heard the boys let out a whoop at the brand-new bow-and-arrow sets their uncle Kane had just bought for them.

"Can we try them out, Dad? Huh? Can we?"

He shot Kane a look that promised retribution for the irresponsible gift. Even if it did say "beginner" on the packaging.

"Maybe tomorrow. We should probably get inside and open the rest of your presents," Luke said, trying to distract them. "We'll have some more cake while we're at it."

"But I thought you said we had to clean up first, Dad?"

"No bows and arrows tonight, guys." Luke ignored their groans. "Besides, it would hurt everyone else's feelings if you played with Uncle Kane's...uh...gift before you even opened theirs."

"Oh, right. Come on, Caden. Let's go."

He watched them race into the house, Kane helping them carry the arrows that hopefully had somewhat blunted tips. Luke took one last look at his kitchen window just in time to see Carmen step away. The arches of his feet tingled and he had a moment of panic before she came back into view, carrying the empty pan of beans.

Yep. She felt like home.

Maybe Drew was right and he could try again. Maybe he could be the kind of man someone like her would deserve. He heard several raised voices, the zinging sound of a released bowstring and then Kane yelled, "Ow. That was my *good* shoulder."

Man, Luke could barely control his own children. Calling him adequate at being a father would be generous. So who was he to say that he'd be any better at a romantic relationship? He remembered his brother's advice and decided there was only one way to find out. Hopefully, he could do so before his wild little monkeys made up Carmen's mind for her.

Carmen hugged herself, unsure of what to do now that most of the cleanup was finished. The boys sat on the floor, tearing into packages as their uncle Drew tried to keep some semblance of order and Mia Mc-Cormick took notes on which person had brought which gift. Cooper and Maxine were drying dishes, and Kylie had just put the girls down to sleep in their portable crib. Luke was sitting on the sofa, having a beer with Alex Russell, while Kane and Hunter worked on a Lego set that was deemed appropriate for ages fourteen and up. The whole scene was too warm, too intimate, too family for Carmen.

She needed to get out of there.

"Hey, kiddos," she finally said, stepping over bows and strewn pieces of torn wrapping paper. "I'm on duty first thing in the morning, so I've got to get home and get some rest. Happy birthday."

She bent down to place a light kiss on each curly blond head.

"Bye, Officer Carmen. Thanks for helping with our party," Aiden said. Then both boys rose up and gave her three hugs, a gesture she'd recently found out Kylie had established with them to help ease their separation anxiety.

"Yeah, thanks, Officer Carmen. It was our bestest birthday ever." Her heart squeezed at Caden's sweet words. Then it dropped at what he said next. "And don't forget to book your room for the tournament next weekend. Choogie said the team hotel in Rexburg will be sold out and if you don't make your reservation, you'll have to stay at the Big Horse Motel down the street. And that one's haunted."

"It's not haunted," Alex said, and all the other adults agreed. "I told you not to listen to Choogie Nguyen. There's no such thing as ghost horses."

"Still, I wouldn't want to stay there and find out," Caden said, sitting back down with his brother and tearing into a gift bag.

"If you can't get a room at the not-haunted hotel, then you could just stay in our room with us," Aiden suggested.

No. She was not staying in a hotel room with them and their father. She rolled her eyes. She wasn't even going to Rexburg in the first place. "Sorry, boys, but I won't be able to make it next weekend."

"But, Officer Carmen, the big tournament starts on Saturday and you've *gotta* go with us. You're our good luck charm. The whole team needs you."

"You guys are great players and you'll try your hardest," Carmen explained. "You don't need me or any luck for that."

The room grew quiet and several Legos fell on the hardwood floor. Actually, Carmen wasn't entirely sure which happened first. But everyone in the room stopped talking, stopped what they were doing and stared at her. Even the twins paused their unwrapping midpresent. "What's wrong? Why's everyone staring at me as if I'm standing on a buried land mine?"

Her answer came from the notoriously quiet Kane Chatterson, who apparently was the only one willing to explain. "You know, Officer Delgado, baseball players are very superstitious. We don't take luck lightly."

They couldn't be serious. She looked around the room. "So you all believe in a person as a good luck charm, but you don't believe in ghost horses?"

Why were they looking at her as though she were the crazy one?

"I can't rightly attest to the goings-on at the Big Horse Motel," Kane continued, speaking for the group. "But I do know baseball. And if the boys and the team think you're good luck, then you are."

"But I'm on duty next weekend," she argued, and saw Luke flinch. What was that about? He couldn't possibly believe his children wouldn't win their game if she wasn't there. Could he?

"Actually," Cooper called out from the kitchen. "You're off on Saturday, and Washington can probably cover your shift on Sunday. Plus, Hunter's team doesn't play until the following weekend, so I'll be on duty while you're gone. The department's got things handled."

Now her boss was assuming she'd just up and leave town for some Little League all-star game? This was utter nonsense. The more she tried to protest, the more everyone insisted she be there. If she argued any more, it would look suspicious. But it wasn't like she could state the real reason she should stay in Sugar Falls.

In fact, she looked straight at that reason, whose eager, smiling expression matched his children's. She really needed to learn how to say no to that ridiculous Gregson dimple.

"Fine. I'll go." The boys cheered while the rest of the room seemed to let out a collective breath. "But I'm getting my own room."

Chapter Ten

Carmen cut off Tim McGraw midchorus as she low-ered the volume of her satellite radio and exited the highway. She'd been raised a big-city girl and, being a cop, she had a pretty good sense of direction. Still, she'd never ventured too far from Sugar Falls and Boise since moving to Idaho and she wanted to con-centrate on where she was driving.

God forbid the good luck charm get lost on her way to the baseball tournament.

Several times this week, the twins had tried to talk her into riding with them and their father to Rexburg. But there was no way, no how, Carmen was allowing herself to be at the mercy of those Gregson males for nearly four hours.

In fact, she'd purposely waited to book a room and was checking last minute prices online for the so-called haunted motel, when Kylie had texted her last night to say she and Drew had to cancel at the last minute because one of the girls had come down with an ear infection. Kylie said the team hotel was booked up, but she could transfer over their reservation. In fact, Kylie had already taken the liberty of calling the hotel and giving them Carmen's name.

She thought some people were going a little overboard in the name of luck for a kids' recreational sports team. But at least Carmen didn't have to share a room with a horse's ghost. Or Luke Gregson. She honestly didn't know which option was less scary.

Probably the former.

After leaving her house at oh six hundred and making two rest stops along the way—damn her weak bladder—Carmen stepped up to the check-in desk at the Springhill Suites with only a few minutes to spare before heading to the ball fields for the first game of a doubleheader.

The lobby was overcrowded with kids wearing ball caps and assorted team jerseys along with the haggard-looking parents who were their chauffeurs, chaperones and cheering sections all in one. Which must've been why she'd had a difficult time hearing the desk clerk explain that there was a notation on her reservation.

"Yoo-hoo, Officer Delgado." Elaine Marconi waved from the other end of the counter. "I barely recognized you in regular clothes. What are you doing here in Rexburg?"

"Just taking in some baseball." Carmen smiled tightly at the woman, not wanting to explain anything else to the town gossip. Then she looked at the clerk, trying to convey her sense of urgency with her eyes as she slid her credit card across the counter. "I'll just take my room key, please."

"Of course, Ms. Delgado. But, as I was explaining, it seems Mr. Gregson has already checked in for you and prepaid for the room. So we won't be needing this." He slid her credit card back toward her.

"Oh, you're here with Luke Gregson." Elaine's magenta-painted lips smirked in a knowing smile.

Had that smug busybody just winked at her? "Oh, no. It's not like that," Carmen tried to explain, but Elaine was busy tapping something into her phone.

"You're in room two-oh-four." The desk clerk handed her a key card. "Your room is adjoining Mr. Gregson's."

Of course, Mrs. Marconi would look up just in time to hear *that* juicy bit of information.

Ugh. Carmen didn't owe this woman or anyone else an explanation. Her head was already pounding and she had a difficult enough time justifying to herself what she was doing at some youth baseball tournament miles away from home.

Besides, she barely had enough time to drop off her suitcase and drive over to the fields if she didn't want all twelve players on the Sugar Falls Comets to blame her for costing them the win.

Her brain hurt, but she managed a pleasant smile as she took the room key and wheeled her small bag toward the elevator as quickly as she could.

By the time she found a parking spot at the crowded park, the boys' team was already taking the field. She scoped out the bleachers and saw the only spot open was next to a woman wearing a pink straw cowboy hat sitting next to an older, shorter version of Luke and Drew Gregson.

No. This couldn't be happening.

"Excuse me." Mrs. Pink Hat waved her fingers to get Carmen's attention. "By any chance are you Officer Carmen?"

With the stands full of fans and parents there to cheer on the team from Sugar Falls, it would've been hard for Carmen to deny it. So she forced herself to smile and nod.

"Here." The woman Carmen suspected was Mrs. Gregson gave her husband a friendly push to make more room. "We've been saving you a seat."

"Hey, Officer Carmen," the shortstop yelled across the field, causing all the players, coaches and spectators to look her way. "My Grammie saved you a seat right next to her and Pop Pop."

If Elaine Marconi hadn't effectively spread the word by now, Aiden or Caden—she couldn't tell which from this distance—had just announced to everyone that Carmen was, in fact, there with the Gregsons.

Like one big happy family.

Coach Alex had repeatedly told the entire team to stay focused on the game. But apparently, Luke wasn't taking those instructions to heart, because he kept peeking over at Carmen when he should have been signaling runners from third base.

He'd seen her several times around town this week, but she'd been working and he hadn't wanted to bother her when she was on duty. Plus, he liked standing back and watching her in her police uniform, all stiff blue polyester and black gear and duty belt. He liked knowing that underneath the bulletproof vest and mirrored sunglasses was a sexy, passionate woman whose skin smelled like gardenias and whose hair smelled like Moroccan oil—whatever that was.

Thanks to the twins, he had her cell phone number programmed in his phone and he could've texted her after the birthday party. But he didn't want to scare her off by coming on too strong. He'd been well aware of her stiff control every time he'd touched her that evening, but he hadn't been able to have her so close and not put his hands on her. He could understand that she probably didn't want everyone to know that their relationship had accelerated directly past the friendship zone and was careening straight toward the romantic expressway.

Luke had been honest with her the other day. His life really was an open book and maybe it was his impulsive and reckless nature, but he didn't like hiding the fact that he was more than attracted to Carmen. The problem was that he couldn't risk a potentially bad outcome, especially publicly.

Again.

At least the twins had been too young to understand what had happened in their parent's marriage or the fact that their father's lack of insight drove their mother into another man's arms. Now, though, the boys were older and would be smart enough to blame him if—or probably when—he messed things up for them.

Even if he'd been willing to listen to Drew's tough-love campaign about him not being the only one at fault, Luke had been lost and racked with guilt for so long, it was instinctive for him to question his judgment about any decision that had to do with his children. And acting on his attraction to Carmen was definitely something that would affect his kids. If he was wrong about where things were heading with her, his selfishness might cause the boys to lose another important woman in their lives.

Which was why it would be easier to avoid any thoughts of a future with Carmen altogether. Unfortunately, judging by the way his mom and dad were yapping in her ear up there in the bleachers, other people were definitely taking an interest in the direction of their relationship, as well.

The team won and the boys had a forty-five minute break to grab a bite to eat before the second game started. Luke was pleased to see that his children ran straight to greet Carmen instead of following the rest of the team to the snack bar. Given the choice between her warm smile and welcoming hug or the standard baseball fare of hot dogs and nachos, he couldn't blame them.

"Did you see the home run I hit, Officer Carmen?" Aiden asked, bouncing up and down on his cleats.

"How about when I got that guy out at third base?" Caden said around a wad of chewing gum. "Did you see *that*?"

"I saw it all, kiddos," Carmen said, then tweaked both their hats. "I was sitting right by Donna and Jerry the whole time."

"You mean Grammie and Pop Pop?" Aiden took both of his grandparents' hands, pulling them toward the snack bar. "They don't like it when we call them Donna and Jerry."

"No, young man," Luke's mom said. "We don't like it when eight—I mean, nine-year-old boys call us by our first names. But Officer Carmen can call us whatever she likes as long as she keeps being your good luck charm."

"No pressure there," Luke thought he heard Carmen mumble.

"See, Officer Carmen." Caden stepped between Luke and Carmen and took them by the hand so they could follow the others. "Everyone knows about your good luckiness. But speaking of nine-year-old boys, Grammie, did you guys maybe remember our birthday just happened last week?"

Luke smiled at Carmen as his parents explained to the children that their birthday presents were still inside the RV, which was parked back at the hotel.

A familiar organ song sounded from the parking lot behind them and Caden squeezed their fingers. "Can we go get something from the ice-cream truck?"

"Sure," Luke said. "But, first, you need to eat something healthy for lunch." Although Luke wasn't seeing many healthy options displayed on the menu board outside the snack bar.

"Okay then, you guys stay here and order us something healthy." Caden put Carmen's hand, which he'd still been holding, into Luke's palm. "Me and Aiden will go get our ice creams before the truck leaves."

With that, the twins took off, leaving Luke and Carmen standing there, linked together.

"Oh, look." Donna Gregson pointed to a food truck that had been set up in the parking lot. "They're selling street tacos. Let's go get those, instead. Jerry and I haven't had any good Mexican food since we left Arizona."

Luke kept Carmen's hand in his own as they followed his parents toward the taco vendor. He'd just spent almost two hours in a dugout with a bunch of rowdy preadolescent boys telling knock-knock jokes and staging a belching contest between innings. If he had to listen to his parents talk about all the roadside diners they'd hit along their travels, then at least Carmen could provide him with a physical distraction.

"So, what's the plan for the rest of the day," Jerry Gregson asked from his spot in line in front of them.

Carmen tried to pull her hand away, but Luke kept his grip firm. "It's a single elimination tournament, so they play again this afternoon. If they win that one, they play again tomorrow morning. The championship game is that same afternoon, but I don't think our team will make it that far. The kids from Sun Valley are pretty good this year."

Luke's mom ordered, then turned back to Carmen. "What are you having, dear?"

"Oh, you don't have to order for me, Mrs. Gregson." At his mom's frown, Carmen corrected herself. "I mean Donna. I can get my own lunch."

"Nonsense. You drove all this way and, from what I understand, you've been great with our grandchildren these past few months. The least Jerry and I can do is buy lunch for—" his mom looked down at their linked hands "—Luke's special friend."

She tried to pull her hand away again, but Luke wasn't having any of it. So, instead, she used his own hand to add momentum as she shoved against his hip.

But Luke didn't budge. "Carmen will have the carnitas, Mom. Extra salsa."

Carmen shoved at him again and twitched her head in the direction of his parents, who were now talking to the woman behind the cash register. He could mentally give himself orders all day long about the inappropriateness of his attraction to her, but it was another thing to make his body obey.

"What?" Luke flashed her a smile, trying to look innocent. "You like things spicy."

"I'm not talking about the salsa, Luke. I'm talking about you paying for my hotel room and now your mom and Elaine Marconi and everyone else back home thinking that we're *special friends*."

He had a feeling that if her fingers hadn't been wedged tightly between his, she would've used air quotes on that last part. "But I thought we *were* friends. And what does Elaine Marconi have to do with anything?"

"She saw me at the hotel and overheard the desk clerk say that you'd already paid for my room."

"I didn't pay for your room. Up until last night, I didn't even know where you were staying. You've been avoiding me all week, remember?"

"I haven't been avoiding you, I've been working. And what do you mean you didn't pay for my room? He clearly said 'Mr. Gregson.' If you don't believe me, ask Elaine. I'm sure she's already telling everyone back in Sugar Falls about it."

"Um, did you ever consider that the *other* Mr. Gregson paid for your room?" Luke asked.

"Your dad?" She squinted her eyes at his father, who was doing a remarkable job of butchering the Spanish language while placing his order. "Why would he pay for it?"

"No, not my dad. My brother, Drew. It was his and Kylie's room originally, remember? He called me last night to say that they couldn't come and were giving you their reservation."

"Oh." Some of the heat left her eyes. "I didn't even think of that."

"Really? And here I thought you were some elite cop with your sexy sunglasses, your tight bun and those fancy interrogation techniques you've been trying to teach me. By the way, I like your hair like this much better."

He reached out his finger and stroked one of the glossy black curls. She jerked her head away, but not before he saw the pink blush streak across her cheeks.

"I know you're teasing me, and normally my investigation skills really are top-notch. But you make it hard for me to think with all your dimpling and high-handedness and...oof." She cut off as he pulled her in closer and wrapped his hand around her waist.

He brought his head down to hers, wanting to show her exactly how high and how low his handedness could reach.

"Two carnitas tacos. Extra salsa," his mother interrupted loudly. Then she lowered her voice and winked before saying, "Save the mushy stuff for later, you two. We're at a family event here."

"This one," his dad said to Carmen, while pointing at Luke, "gets his moves from his old man." Jerry Gregson then spun his wife toward him and dipped her into his arms, extra salsa and all, before planting a big kiss on her laughing lips.

That was what Luke had grown up with. That was the kind of easy, lighthearted relationship he'd always wanted for himself. But seeing Carmen's forced smile, feeling her suddenly tense up against him... It was beginning to occur to him that his instincts had been wrong again. And that maybe she didn't want the same things. Or at least, not with someone like him.

That evening, Carmen sat next to Luke on the wooden bench in the pizza parlor, her appetite slowly returning to compete with her building frustration at the man for being so damn sexy and funny. The team had stopped for dinner on the way back to the hotel and there was no sense in her going hungry all alone in her prepaid hotel room.

She'd finally convinced herself to just have a slice of the sausage-and-mushroom pie, maybe even loosen up enough to allow herself to relax and enjoy Luke's playfulness and close proximity.

Temporarily.

Yet, now that she'd ordered herself not to fight it, she could sense that something was off. Luke's arm was touching hers, but he hadn't been as blatantly affectionate since that stunt he'd pulled earlier today.

Maybe the fun for him was in sneaking the touches and kisses and whatnot—like he was getting away with something or trying to get her rattled. If he was anything like his offspring—and she was quickly realizing that he was—the man had a penchant for getting himself into borderline mischievous situations. But now that the nonsecret was out of the bag, perhaps the game for him was over.

Carmen had known plenty of men who were only interested in the chase. While Luke seemed comfortable flirting with her, the fact remained that he was still not over his late wife. Maybe he was having some guilt over this make-believe one-big-happy-family situation he'd gotten himself into.

"Dad, did you pack our swimsuits?" Caden yelled, popping his curly blond head out of the arcade room.

"I sure did, Caden." Luke smiled at his son and Carmen forgot about relaxing. Who could relax when seeing the man's dimples felt like the carbonation from her soda was bubbling around in her chest? "Remember, you reminded me about eight times?

"The kids have been talking about the hotel's indoor pool all day," Luke said, finally breaking the awkward silence between them. Was he trying to make small talk?

"I know," she replied, remembering the message she'd gotten from Luke's cell phone, which turned out not to be from Luke at all. "Aiden texted me on Wednesday telling me to pack my own bathing suit." And she had, because, sure, she liked a good swim. And up until now, she'd done whatever the sweet boys had asked. But that was before everyone suspected that she and Luke were involved.

"I really need to figure out a way to keep those boys away from other people's phones."

Was he annoyed that his kids were talking to her more regularly and had invited her on this trip? She sat up straighter. Or maybe he just wanted her opinion on how to establish better boundaries. If so, he was talking to the wrong person.

She watched the other parents round up their children to leave the restaurant and go back to the hotel for the night. Despite working in a male-dominated occupation for years, she'd never felt so out of place as she did now. She was used to being the one in charge, the one making the commands, yet seeing the moms wiping pizza-smeared faces and herding kids wired on soda and video games, Maria Carmen Delgado was at a complete loss.

She felt like a fraud. She wasn't a mom, and she never would be. She shouldn't be playing up some happy little family role or pretending that things could continue on like this.

In fact, at some point this weekend, she needed a one-on-one with Luke to explain to him that *nothing* was happening between them. Well, technically, something had already happened, but it needed to stop there. They weren't in a relationship; nor was she planning to enter into one with him.

No matter how stinking adorable he was when he lifted up his sons, one in each muscular arm, and carried their giggling little bodies out of the restaurant and toward the parking lot.

"Can we ride back to the hotel with you, Officer Carmen?" the boys begged in unison, and all her tough resolve melted like the mozzarella cheese they'd all just consumed.

"If it's okay with your father," she said, wanting to make the point that she wasn't their parent. She didn't get to make these kinds of decisions about them, no matter how much she might want to.

"Make sure you wear your seat belts," Luke said. And don't ask her to stop at that ice-cream parlor we passed on the way here."

Carmen loaded the boys into her SUV and, as she pulled onto the main road, she saw that Luke followed in the Nanamobile with his parents. Which made it impossible to give in to the twin's requests for ice cream without getting busted.

After their failed attempts, Caden switched tactics. "So, when we get to our rooms, Officer Carmen, you go get your swimsuit on and we'll give you the secret knock to let you know we're ready."

The secret knock? "What secret knock?"

"Like this." Aiden demonstrated four quick raps on the window, followed by two bangs, then a tapping of fingers.

"Oh, of course. *That* secret knock. Actually, boys, I'm pretty tired from the long drive today. I think I'm going to skip the pool and just go to bed."

"But how can you be tired, Officer Carmen?" Aiden asked. "You didn't even hafta play baseball today. You just got to sit there and watch us do all the work."

"I'll have you both know that being a good luck charm requires a lot of focus and concentration." And nerves of steel to be questioned so thoroughly by Donna Gregson during the second ball game. The woman could teach a training class at the Military Police School. "I wasn't able to use the restroom or get up and walk around at all for fear you guys might lose the lead. That's a lot of work, you know."

The boys conferred in the backseat. "Maybe you're right. In that case, you should come with us to the pool and sit in the hot tub. Choogie Nguyen said we have to be fourteen to go in the hot tub because it's for adults only who want to relax."

"Oh, you guys. I think my room will be more re-laxing than the pool."

More nine-year-old whispers.

"All right then, Officer Carmen. We'll just skip the

pool and come hang out with you in your room so we can *all* relax. Together. We have a big game tomorrow and need to be ready for it."

"We found the pay-per-view channel and Dad said we couldn't get the new space robots movie because it would give him nightmares. But maybe if we open that door between our rooms, we can come watch it in yours. If Dad hears it and gets scared, we'll tell him you're there to protect us. It'll be like having a sleepover. But with a gun. You *did* bring your gun, didn't you, Officer Carmen?"

Suddenly, her evening plans were sounding about as relaxing as a nighttime airstrike in the Afghani desert.

She steered her car into the hotel parking lot and saw—or rather heard—Luke pull into the space alongside her. He really needed to get that muffler checked—it was roaring so loud she needed earplugs. "You know what, kiddos. Let's just go to the pool, after all. I think your friend Choogie is right about the hot tub being more relaxing."

She wasn't sure, but the smacking sound she heard coming from her backseat sounded suspiciously like a high five. But before she could chastise the two little manipulators, they swung her door open, banging it into the side of the Nanamobile. She cringed, but figured the sturdy vehicle wouldn't be affected much.

"Easy there, monkey," Luke said to his son, who was already running with his brother toward the hotel entrance. He examined Carmen's back passenger door for dings. "I don't think there's any dents. You want to come over here and have a look?"

No. No, she absolutely did not want to stand that

close to Luke and have a look at anything. Especially not the way the dim orange glow from the parking lot lighting made him look even more golden, if that was possible—like a damn sexy golden angel, when she knew her thoughts about him were anything but angelic.

"I'm sure it's fine," she said, then coughed to clear the raspiness from her throat. "Besides, the twins are over there pushing a couple of their teammates into the lobby on the luggage cart. You better go after them."

She watched Luke sprint and dodge several cars to catch up with his sons. It would've been comical if she hadn't been transfixed by the muscular definition in his legs as he ran.

Instead of teaching a kickboxing class, she should've specialized in yoga; maybe that way she would've learned how to take more calming breaths. As it was, Carmen took her time walking and breathing and trying not to think of the man who set her pulse racing one minute and her brain skidding to a stop the next.

She made it to her room just in time to overhear Luke chastising the twins from next door. His firm voice promised that if there were any more shenanigans, they wouldn't be going swimming tonight. Not that she wanted the boys to be in trouble, but she'd honestly been hoping for a slight reprieve.

This was fast becoming the uncomfortable day that would never end. Even in her most depressed days of painful recuperation from her hysterectomy, she hadn't been this emotionally miserable, knowing her life was changing for the worse.

She massaged the scar tissue below her belly button. Hey. Maybe that was what she should do. Carmen looked at the two-piece bathing suit she'd thrown into her suitcase at the last minute. When she'd packed early this morning, her tired brain had instructed her hand to just grab the first thing available. She'd recalled Aiden's text to pack a swimsuit and she'd grabbed both of hers, not planning to participate in any group activities besides attending the games.

Yet, now she needed to decide. Should she wear the functional one-piece and cover up her scars? Or should she put it all out there and let Luke—and everyone else—see what she'd been hiding for far too long?

Carmen knew when to retreat—and when to draw her battle lines.

Hearing the anxious chatter next door, she realized the clock was ticking. She wiggled into the suit and paused to look at herself in the bathroom mirror. At least she'd been somewhat modest when she'd originally purchased the two-piece, back when she and Mark had been planning their first vacation together. The bottoms provided plenty of coverage and the halter top kept the girls firmly in place. The only thing the bathing suit actually revealed was her abdomen.

Rap, rap, rap, rap. Bang, bang. Tap, tap, tap, tap.

The designated knock sounded on the adjoining door, but she refused to open it. That thin plywood barrier was her last line of defense from the intimacy of the Gregson family, and she wasn't about to give it up.

"I'll meet you guys in the hallway," she called out before grabbing a cotton sundress she'd packed as an impromptu cover-up.

When Carmen walked out of her room, she tried

not to stare at Luke's board shorts, the same ones he'd been wearing when she'd helped pull them out of the river by her cottage. Instead, she and Luke followed the two boys as they bounced off the hallway walls all the way downstairs to the indoor pool.

She looked at the clock on the wall. It was almost eight o'clock and the small pool was filled to near capacity with shouting children doing cannonballs, shooting water guns and splashing each other silly.

She offered to get them towels and was setting all their belongings on an empty chaise longue when the boys made a mad dash into the overcrowded pool. Deliberately turning her back to Luke, she took off her dress, though she could feel his eyes on her when she finally, slowly turned around.

This was it. The moment of truth.

Chapter Eleven

Thankfully, the whirlpool was nearly empty, hosting only a pair of goggles, a few toddler toys and an abandoned water wing. Luke whistled through his teeth as he dipped a toe into the heated water. No wonder the kids were avoiding this particular location. Well, that and the big sign posted on the wall that read Adults Only.

He had already stripped off his shirt and was soaking in the hot tub when he saw Carmen pull her dress over her head. Thankfully, he was halfway submerged under water because he couldn't control his body's reaction to her curves.

He'd known plenty of beautiful women, including his wife. But there was something different about Carmen. She was strong, athletic and capable of probably anything. Was there anything more alluring than that?

She walked toward Luke, her gaze locked straight

on his, and it felt like she was moving just for him, just to gauge his reaction to her perfectly proportioned and very female shape. Luke was so overwhelmed with desire he couldn't even manage to smile.

Boing. A wet plastic football hit him right in the temple.

"Sorry, Captain Gregson," Choogie Nguyen, the know-it-all teammate, said as he ran over to retrieve the ball. The twins were right behind him.

"Wow, Officer Carmen, you got a lot of lines on your tummy," Caden said when he plopped his little wet body on the cement by them.

Prompted by his son's comment, Luke allowed his eyes to roam across Carmen's body. He spotted a few scars on her lower abdomen. Those were probably nasty wounds at one point. Still, that didn't make his son's rude observation okay.

Luke touched the boy's shoulder in gentle reproach. "Caden, you're being very impolite."

"No, that's okay," Carmen said. "He's just being observant. You're right, kiddo. I *do* have a lot of lines on my tummy. They're scars."

"Lemme see," Aiden said, jostling in beside his brother.

Carmen stood on the second step of the hot tub, allowing his brashly curious children to look at her.

"How'd you get them?"

"When I was a police officer in Las Vegas, a very bad man didn't want me to arrest him. So he stabbed me."

"Oh, cool," Choogie said.

"Actually, it wasn't cool at the time. It hurt very badly."

"Did you shoot the bad guy dead?" Caden wanted to know.

"No," Carmen said patiently. She was clearly uncomfortable talking about this, yet she wore a brave face for his children. Luke should've stopped the questions, but, like his boys, he was just as curious. "I wrestled his knife away."

"While you were bleeding?" All three pairs of nine-year-old eyes were wide open, starstruck.

Carmen nodded. "That's my job."

"You're pretty tough for a girl," Choogie said.

"She's pretty tough for anyone," Luke corrected. "Okay, you guys. Give Officer Carmen some space and let her relax."

He waved the kids off, laughing as they tried to outdo each other's belly flops into the pool. Luke turned back to Carmen, who had put on her Officer Controlling mask again as she sank into the jet bubbles. He noticed she did it whenever she didn't want to be asked any personal questions.

Or maybe she did it because she wanted to express to him in no uncertain terms that she was off-limits. He'd been out of practice too long so it was possible he'd misread her patience for attraction. It could also be that she'd spent enough time with the wild monkeys he called children and decided she wanted nothing to do with the three-for-one package deal.

Before, he'd thought her aloofness was simply because she was reserved, and he'd been careful but playful with his displays of affection. Yet, this afternoon, he'd taken a step back, like Drew always cautioned him to do, and tried to see things more rationally.

Up until recently, Luke had doubted that he'd ever get over his perceived role in Samantha's death. But in the dark recesses of his mind—where he'd pushed back the possibility of finding someone to share his life with—he knew that he couldn't be with a woman who didn't love his children as much as he did. He was pretty sure Carmen loved the boys. After all, nobody could fake that kind of patience and tolerance for their antics.

Which brought him back full circle. If it wasn't the twins, it must be him.

He hated to give up so easily, to abandon a mission once he'd taken it on. But he wasn't going to force Carmen into a relationship or anything else she so clearly wasn't comfortable with.

So it looked like he needed to tamp down his impulsiveness. Get used to this whole friends idea she'd suggested that day they went shopping. Being friends was better than nothing.

Not wanting to stare at her, he tried to focus on his surroundings. The room housing this indoor pool was packed and had acoustics that must be echoing the shrieking and splashing kids throughout the rest of the hotel. Yet, the silence between the two of them was deafening.

"It's been a long day," Luke said, wanting to make small talk. Or any kind of talk.

"It really has," she answered. But instead of looking relaxed, she looked more keyed up than she had all day. In fact, she looked like she was on high alert.

"You look as if you're waiting for a criminal to burst in and burglarize the swimming area."

"I think a burglar would take one peek inside this

madhouse and start running." She nodded toward a group of kids staging a chicken fight of UFC proportions.

"Boys," Luke yelled when he saw what was going on in the shallow end. "No wrestling in the pool. It's dangerous."

When they leaped out of the water to chase one of their teammates, Carmen added, "And no running."

He watched the boys slow down to a speed walk, not surprised that they were quick to obey her directions. "They respond really well to you."

"They're good kids. They have good hearts."

He wanted to tell her that he had a good heart, too. But so what? Other than that, he didn't have much to offer a woman.

"They've gotten really close to you," he said.

"I know." She sighed. Was that a good sigh or a bad sigh? Luke couldn't tell. "I worry that maybe we've gotten too attached to each other."

"We? You mean you and me?"

"Actually, I was talking about me and the kids," she said, making his chest sink like the toy anchor at the bottom of the hot tub. "Listen, Luke. I really need to tell you something. To explain why—"

"Hold that thought," Luke interrupted, seeing his mom waving at him from the doorway. Carmen whipped her head around, the black curls piled on top of her head threatening to spill into the water. "The boys are sleeping in the RV with my parents tonight and I need to get them out and dried off before Mom and Dad change their minds."

She held her mouth in a tiny O of surprise. And if he wasn't sure where her conversation had been headed, he would've been tempted to kiss the surprise right off her lips. But he really did need to get his kids out of here before Carmen delivered her big thanks-but-no-thanks speech, which would end up breaking more than one Gregson heart.

"Give me two minutes," he said, rising out of the water. "Then we can finish talking about this."

Carmen followed Luke to where they'd left their dry stuff, trying not to stare at the way the droplets of water trailed down to the back of his narrow waist.

Not that she wanted to have this conversation in front of the children, but she'd liked the idea of having them nearby as sort of an added buffer in case they needed a quick change of topic. Or in case Luke smiled at her and made her rethink this whole exit strategy.

She grabbed a towel, unable to stave off the chill that had entered her well before she'd exited the hot tub.

"You know what," she said, pulling her cotton dress on over her wet bathing suit. "We can talk tomorrow. I'm just going to head back to my room now, anyway."

"Chicken," Luke whispered as the boys came running over to get their towels.

"See you tomorrow morning, Dad," they said, giving him three hugs. Then they turned to Carmen, pressing their wet bodies against her and counted out three hugs for her, as well.

Aiden and Caden were all the way to the door and walking out with their grandmother before Carmen could ask Luke to repeat what he'd just said.

"I called you a chicken," he said. The childish flapping of his pretend wings only served to draw her attention to the rest of his very adult and very real body.

"You think I'm scared of something, Gregson?" She shoved her toes into her flip-flops, the force of one foot causing the sandal to flip over. So much for a smooth exit strategy.

"I think that when you use my last name, you're scared. Or pissed. Or maybe both."

She looked around at the other parents and children still frolicking in the pool well past closing time. She was not about to do this right here.

"Fine. You want to talk, let's go talk." She finally got her shoe on and strode to the glass doors, not waiting to see if he'd follow. Or looking down at the damp towel directly in her path. She stumbled and was somewhat surprised that he was close enough to wrap his arm around her and pull her up against him.

Dammit. Why was he always doing that? The only secure thing she liked around her waist was her gun belt.

"Your room or mine?" Luke asked when they got into the hotel hallway leading toward the elevator.

"What?" She pulled back and jerked her head in his direction. The guy couldn't be serious. Did he really think she was about to jump into bed with him?

"You know that conversation you started and then changed your mind about when you got scared?" he asked. "I'm guessing that you don't want to give me the brush-off in front of a lobby full of witnesses. So whose room do you want to talk in? Mine or yours?"

She couldn't really see how he could call it a brush-off when nothing had really started between them in the first place. At least not yet. But the fact that he was thinking about them in terms of a potential relationship made her more determined to put an end to things before he got his expectations up.

"I guess we should go back to your room," she said, right as the elevator door opened to reveal Elaine Marconi carrying an ice bucket and a smile of delight at what she'd just overheard.

"No kids?" Elaine asked, then giggled. "Have a fun night, you two."

Luke smiled at the smug woman before she did a knowing finger wave and toddled off toward where a few of the other moms were sitting in the lobby with a couple of open bottles of wine.

Ugh. Carmen stepped into the elevator and tried to push the door-close button before Luke was even inside.

"Why'd you dimple her?" she asked, hating the accusing tone in her voice.

"Why did I *what* her?"

"Dimple. You dimpled her."

"What in the heck does that mean?"

"You smile with those cute, sneaky dimples anytime you're trying to get out of trouble or act all innocent. I saw you do it with Nurse Dunn a couple of weeks ago when Caden faked sick to get out of his spelling test and she told you he'd need a doctor's note saying he didn't have poison oak before he would be allowed to return to class. And you do it to me every chance you get."

"I can't help it," Luke said. "It's reflexive. Probably because I get into trouble a lot." His eyes looked down at the two wet triangle shapes outlined on her dress. "Does it work?"

"Only on women who don't know any better." The elevator doors dinged open and she walked out.

"And you know better?" he said, catching up to her and pulling his room key out of the hidden pocket in his board shorts.

She really needed to stop looking at him and the way the thin, damp material rode so low on his hips. *You're a cop, Delgado. Toughen up.* "It's my job to know trouble when I see it."

He slid his key in the electronic lock and she glanced next door, thinking it wasn't too late to avoid this whole thing and go straight to her own room.

But, like she'd told herself earlier, she wasn't a coward. Still, this was scarier than serving an arrest warrant at a gun show. She was trained in tactical procedures, but no amount of training could keep her heart from being blasted apart.

She followed him into his suite, only to be hit with an icy blast of air-conditioning. "Man, I told those boys not to mess with the A/C unit this morning," Luke said as he walked over and fiddled with the small control panel on the wall. "They think anything with a display screen is as much fun as an arcade game. I guess I should've reset the timer when we came back to get changed for the pool."

When he turned back to her, she could see that his bare torso was covered in gooseflesh, his dark pink nipples as tight as her own. And, apparently, despite the layers of wet fabric she was wearing, he could see the same thing.

Luke took a step toward her. Then another. She recognized the desire in his eyes because it probably mirrored her own. Carmen's back was now pressed against the wall, literally and figuratively.

"I can't have kids." Carmen heard the words but had no idea why she'd blurted them out. It must've been the safest thing she could think to say.

"What?" Luke froze, then shook his head, as though he could shake off her poorly timed admission. She would almost have laughed at the expression on his face if the whole situation hadn't been so sadly disappointing. He sure wasn't dimpling her now.

She decided to take advantage of his confusion and gain the upper hand. "I said I can't have kids."

"I know what you said." Even though his ears had apparently heard it, his eyes were asking *why* she'd said it in the first place.

"You know my scars?" she asked, trying to start over.

"What scars?"

"The ones I just showed you by the pool?" She waited for some sort of acknowledgment, but he just stood there, looking baffled.

Although, in his defense, she'd just blindsided him with an unexpected revelation. She'd been in the surgical recovery room when Mark had first found out, but she imagined her ex must have had the same reaction.

She yanked her damp dress off over her head, causing the knot of curls to come loose. She pushed several loose strands of hair out of her face and pointed to her bared midriff.

He glanced at her abdomen quickly before blatantly staring at every other part of her body. Was he too disgusted to look at that them?

"What about your scars?" he said, once his eyes

had made their way back down. "We all have them. You aren't self-conscious about them, are you?"

"No. I can't have children because of them." She heard the catch in her voice and realized it was the first time she'd ever said it out loud. Well, not counting the first two times just a minute ago when Luke obviously hadn't understood her. Now, she needed to make him understand. "I was stabbed multiple times. My armored vest protected me from any fatal injuries, but the guy got me right here." She held one hand under her belly button and the other right above the top of her swimsuit bottom. "The knife punctured my uterus. During my emergency surgery, they had to do a complete hysterectomy."

But Luke must've heard, because his confused face relaxed into tenderness and he angled his head and walked toward her. "Aw, sweetheart, I'm sorry."

His thumb skimmed against the biggest, ugliest ridge of flesh before he spread his hands along her waist and pulled her toward him. He kissed her temple and wrapped an arm around her.

She smelled the slight tang of chlorine on his shoulder as she buried her face in his neck. She felt his hand move from her waist up to stroke her back, and a sob she'd thought was nonexistent rose up through her chest and slipped out her throat before she could reel it back in.

Maria Carmen Delgado was not a crier. Especially not in front of good-looking macho men who might mistake her tears for a sign of weakness.

And she'd never felt more weak in her life. She stood in Luke's arms, in his warm and safe embrace, and cried for every time she'd been told that she couldn't do something because she was a woman, for every time that she'd had to sacrifice a small piece of herself—of her femininity—for a career that she loved. But, mostly, she cried for the unfulfilled dream of motherhood that she'd never get to experience.

If her body was shaking with sobs, she couldn't feel them. Luke held her in a cocoon of strength, allowing her outside to be safely protected while the inside of her raged with frustration and sadness.

But as her eyes dried up and his tender reassuring strokes became more sensual, more arousing, she forced herself to push him away.

"Are you okay?" he asked, his face still way too close to hers.

She nodded. "Sorry about that. I don't usually get so emotional."

"It's okay to have feelings, Carmen. You don't have to be a cop all the time."

"I know, but it's a safe role for me. Anyway, thanks for… Well, thanks for whatever that was." She couldn't bring herself to express gratitude for holding her up when she was completely breaking down. She'd already suffered the indignity of admitting her deepest injury, her biggest regret, and then crying about it while he patted her back and told her everything would be okay.

But it wasn't okay. And it never would be. She'd officially hammered in the final nail to the "just friends" coffin. This is when most men would give her the brush-off. But because she'd put herself into the power position, she could walk away with at least some of her pride intact.

Not much. But some.

She wiped her cheek with the back of her hand, making sure any traces of her tearful breakdown were gone. She couldn't help the small sniffle as she turned her head to the side, looking at the door.

"So I'm going to go pack up my things. Tell the boys that I had to get back to Sugar Falls, but I'm sure they'll play great even if I'm not there."

She didn't bother picking up her cotton dress as she made her way toward the door. She was walking out of all of their lives and it was best not to look back.

Chapter Twelve

"Wait? You're leaving?" Luke was incredulous. "In your bikini?"

"I'm just wearing it next door. I'll get dressed before I go."

"But why are you suddenly taking off?" Was he asking the wrong questions? He wanted to stamp his feet in frustration because he'd just held the woman and told her everything would be okay. So why wasn't she listening to him?

She held the door open but turned back to look at him. "Luke, didn't you just hear me? Were you not paying attention?"

"Oh, I was paying attention all right. How can a man not pay attention when you're standing there in that—" he gestured at the two-piece bathing suit "—with your hair all…?" He used both hands to motion at the sexy, tousled mess of curls.

"Then what part aren't you getting?"

"The part where you're *leaving*."

"I just told you why." She folded her arms across her chest, a stance he'd seen her take when she was reprimanding the twins or busy explaining to Scooter and Jonesy why they couldn't ride their horses down Snowflake Boulevard and through the center of town.

"No, you didn't. You showed me some scars and said some ass stabbed you." Luke drew in a deep breath and let it out slowly. "I said I was sorry. And then I held you while you cried. Did I do something wrong?"

"No, Luke. You did everything right," she accused, looking like she was about to cry again. "That's the problem."

Dammit. Where was Drew's analytical and rational thinking when Luke needed it the most? "Okay." He finally latched on to an idea. "Remember when you talked Caden down off the cafeteria rafters? I'm going to need you to talk me down here, because I'm still not getting it."

"I can't have children. And you want more children. Which means that I can't have you. I'm trying to do the honorable thing here and walk away."

"When did I say that I wanted to have more children? Have you met the ones I already have? They're a handful."

"You said it that night at Patrelli's, when you and the twins were picking up pizza for poker night. You told me the next children you had would have better manners."

"Carmen, I also said that it was okay for my son to pretend his ACE bandage was a real cast. I was trying to be funny and lighten the mood. It was the first time

I'd seen you out of uniform and I was too busy staring down your shirt to think about what I was saying."

A bubble of laughter escaped her lips. "I *knew* you were staring down my shirt, but you flashed those damn dimples and I thought it was just wishful thinking on my part."

He tried smiling at her again. "Sweetheart, I'll stare down your shirt whenever you want if you'll just come back inside."

"Oh, my." Luke heard a woman's voice down the hall, followed by a chorus of giggles. He saw Elaine Marconi and Choogie Nguyen's moms enjoying the drama unfolding in the hotel hallway.

"Come on," he said as he pulled a bikini-clad Carmen into his room.

He allowed the door to slam closed before chancing a look at the pink blush staining her cheeks. He needed to understand this woman. He needed to have a rational and logical conversation with her without his hormones getting in the way.

"So, to clarify, you're telling me you don't want to date me because you can't have children?"

"It's not that I don't want to, Luke. It's that it'd be unfair to you."

Did she just say unfair? He'd been beating himself up over whether he should tell this woman how he felt about her, but now that she'd initiated the conversation, he was going to use his SEAL logic and get comfortable being uncomfortable. To hell with rational thinking and common sense. He was going back to impulsive and reckless.

"You know what's unfair?" he asked. "It's unfair that you look at me with all that heat and passion and then put up emotional barricades every time I try to get close to you. It's unfair that your bathroom full of soaps and lotions and beauty products has officially ruined me from ever enjoying a shower again because all I can think about is the smell of your hair and the softness of your skin. It's unfair that you were right about taking your bigger car to Costco and how much potato salad to make for a birthday party, because you know how to do these things and I don't. It's unfair that you were the one who could talk Caden down from the cafeteria rafters and I just sat there eating a pudding cup because I never know what to say. It's unfair for you to come into my children's lives and love them as much as any mother could while I burn dinners and accidentally wave them on to home plate because I'm too busy staring at you in the stands to be a decent third-base coach." He stared at her, hot, angry—desperate. "And it's unfair for you to let me hold you while you're wearing that incredibly sexy bathing suit and then walk away without at least a goodbye kiss."

Before she could look down to confirm what she was wearing, he dipped his head to hers and kissed her with all the reckless disregard of a hopeless man hanging by a snapped cable out of a helicopter over the ocean. She was his harness, his lifeline, and he needed to hold on to her and scramble to save himself.

He paused for only a second, just long enough for her to push him away if she still wanted out of this. Instead, he felt her fingers course over his scalp and then to the back of his neck as she pulled his head in closer, his kiss in deeper.

Luke moaned and allowed his hands to roam freely

across her skin, which was smoother and warmer than it'd been ten minutes ago. He reached the clasp at the back of her bathing suit top and unhooked it, sliding his thumbs under the elastic strap as it released its hold on her.

He followed the lines of the loosened fabric around to the front, where he was able to cup her breasts. Her perfect, round breasts that he'd been thinking about ever since that night at Patrelli's. As she moved her tongue in and out of his mouth, taking advantage of everything he was offering, he used his thumbs and forefingers to massage her nipples into tighter peaks.

Carmen gasped and pressed against him more, causing him to take a step back. She didn't release his mouth as she brought her arms down and gripped his hips. At first, Luke relished in the pleasure of her pushing against him, but soon he realized that Carmen was actually walking him backward.

Toward the bed.

They were both used to being in control, but Luke had been waiting for this for so long he didn't want to give her the upper hand. He bent his head lower, kissing a trail down her neck and toward her chest. By the time he had his tongue on her nipple, he also had rotated their positions and maneuvered her against the down-filled comforter.

But she was quicker and hooked one of her legs around the back of his knee, then leveraged herself so that when she pushed against his shoulders, he turned to his left before collapsing on the bed.

"Nice takedown maneuver," Luke said, before reaching for her waist and pulling her down on top of him.

"I prefer being in the power position," Carmen said as she straddled her long legs on either side of him.

"So do I," he replied before flipping her onto her back, then fitting himself perfectly between her open legs.

He kissed her again and she lifted her body to meet his demand.

"Tell me you want this," he said, pressing the ridge of his erection against the thin fabric of her bikini bottoms.

"I want this," she admitted, wrapping her legs around his hips.

"Do we need protection?" he asked. Then he realized his mistake as he felt her grow not just still, but cold in his arms.

His words felt as though he'd just dumped that stupid ice bucket on her. "I thought I made it pretty clear that I couldn't get pregnant."

"You did. And I'm not worried about that," he said before pulling back and dropping to the bed beside her, his arm covering his eyes. "Man, there's no good way to talk about this."

The air-conditioning vent kicked back on, making Carmen aware that she was almost naked and lying in bed with a man she should've said goodbye to a month ago. She tried to tug at the sheets, but the six-foot-four man was planted firmly in the middle of the bed. She was tempted to at least grab a pillow and use it to shield herself. But that would only cover her nudity. Not her shame.

"We don't need to talk about anything," she said as she sat up and looked around for her bathing suit top.

"Where are you going?"

Carmen was surprised he'd had to ask. "Back to my room. Home."

"But I thought you said you wanted this."

"I *do* want this. But I know I can't have it."

"Are we back to that whole you-can't-have-children thing? Because that's not what I meant about using protection."

"Then what did you mean?"

"Look, I know this is going to make me sound unmanly and way out of practice, but I haven't been with a woman since Samantha died."

Oh, no. He wasn't over his wife. She hoped that the room was too dark for him to see the way her lungs trembled with her indrawn breath.

"I understand," she said, before standing up.

"Wait. You're trying to leave again?" His reflexes were quicker than she'd expected and he hauled her back toward the bed and had his arm wrapped around her waist before she'd even taken a step.

"Luke, even if you claim you're fine not having any more kids, it's pretty obvious you still love your wife. I could never compete against the mother of your children." She felt ridiculous, admitting this while he was practically spooning her. Could she have allowed herself to be put in any weaker a position? Both physically and emotionally?

"There's no competition," he said. But even with the assertive tone of his voice, Carmen still had her doubts. She tried to wedge an elbow behind her as leverage for getting back up.

"Why do you do that?" he asked, pulling her in tighter.

"Do what?" She stiffened, even though she knew she should be relaxing her body in order to get away.

"Try to tell me what I'm saying and then make a break for it and run off before I can even correct you."

"I'm not trying to run off." She couldn't see his face, but she was pretty sure his eyebrows were raised in doubt.

"Yes, you are. It's like you retreat before the battle can be fought."

"What battle?"

"This battle." His arm pulled her in tighter. "The one between the two of us." But instead of feeling locked in, she actually felt safe. Like she wasn't fighting this alone.

"It's called self-preservation."

"What do you need to protect yourself from?"

"From getting hurt," she admitted. Even saying as much made her weaker.

"I'm not going to hurt you, Carmen. I'm trying to love you. But you have to clue me in on the rules of engagement."

His words made her feel lighter, but slightly more vulnerable—as if she'd stripped off her Kevlar vest before her duty shift had ended. "I didn't ask you to try and love me."

"I know. I stupidly undertook that risky operation all on my own."

Hearing him refer to himself as *stupid* caused her feeling of being weak to fall by the wayside. Suddenly, his words were clicking into place. "Are you saying that you love me?"

"Yes, woman. What the hell do you think I've been trying to show you for the past hour?"

Her rib cage tightened and her spine tingled, and it felt like all the fluttering butterflies inside her body had just declared mutiny and were demanding their freedom. She held still, only allowing her head to tilt slightly back so she could see the earnestness on his face.

"Listen, Carmen, I get that you've been hurt and that your life plans probably got all kinds of jacked up by that knife attack. But how could you think any of that would matter to a man who loves you?"

"Mark loved me, but it mattered to him. He was relieved when I broke up with him."

"Are you talking about the idiot who married your cousin? Please tell me you're not comparing me to him."

"Luke, I've been around men all my life. Brothers, relatives, coworkers—I'm surrounded by them all the time. I know what they want and I know how to read them."

"Well, you read me all wrong then, sweetheart. Because I want *you*. Not your reproductive organs or what you can provide me, but you. Just you."

He brushed a kiss along her lips, and Carmen wanted to open back up to him again. Then she remembered something.

"What about Samantha?"

"What about her?"

"You aren't still carrying a torch for her?"

Luke sighed. "I can't change the fact that I once loved her. But I was also a very different man when I was married to her." He paused, looking away for a moment, then went on, "I thought marriage and having children would ground me, settle me down. This may be hard for you to believe, but I'd always been the wild twin, the reckless one who got into trouble every time I turned around. Drew was the calm one, always thinking things through, and even though it was more fun to be naughty, I envied that. Getting married and doing the responsible thing made me feel more like him. I loved that feeling. But when she died, I no longer felt grounded. I don't know if that's because I'd lost that sense of security or because I'd lost her. Honestly, we never spent enough time together to give our relationship a chance."

"But the twins were three when she died. That's longer than you've known me."

"True, but I was away on deployments a lot of the time. We met at a bar one night, through mutual friends. I'm not proud of this, but what I thought was a one-night stand ended up as a pregnancy and a quickie wedding in Vegas in between duty assignments. We got along well enough and she handled everything when it came to the twins. Looking back on it, she probably took on all the responsibility of raising them because she felt insecure in our relationship. And I allowed her to because I was busy running off to save the world and didn't have to worry about it."

"Was that why you asked about protection earlier?" Carmen bit her bottom lip, not sure she wanted to know the answer. "Because of what happened the last time you had a one-night stand?"

"First of all, in case I haven't made it clear, this thing between you and me is *not* a one-night stand." Carmen's tummy did a little flip. "Second of all, I asked about protection because my commanding officer once read us the riot act about the possibility of diseases. I'm clean, just for the record."

"That's good to know," Carmen said, thinking that was really the least of her worries. "I am, too. Just for the record."

He smiled, and pulled her leg up and over him. "So now that you know about all my failings, I'll try not to stop you if you want to leave."

"I think your grip on my thigh says otherwise. But what failings would those be?"

"I don't always trust my judgment when it comes to knowing what a woman wants. I wasn't the man Samantha wanted me to be and I carried around a lot of guilt about her death. It still resurfaces from time to time."

"But why was it your fault?"

"I wasn't around a lot during my marriage. And Samantha was under a lot of stress with the twins and my deployments and handling everything on her own. It wasn't until I mentioned something to my brother about it the other day that I started to rethink things."

"Didn't she have anyone to help her? I know the military has programs in place to assist dependents."

"That's what Drew had pointed out, too. But then I added to that by volunteering for every dangerous mission under the sun. I felt like I'd failed as a husband, and therefore, I would eventually fail as a father."

"But, Luke, you're a great father."

He shook his head. "I try. I'm still getting my bearings, but I'm scared to death that I'm going to do something to mess it all up. I changed assignments last summer so that I can be around all the time now, but it's been a learning curve. My family has helped me so much, but when you took on the twins for that mentorship program..." He swiped his hand over his eyes, then cleared his throat. "Well, you'll never know how much I appreciate you being there for them."

"Are you kidding? I feel like *I'm* the one who benefited. I left my family and moved here knowing I would be all alone, with no hope of ever having children of my own. I was scared to death that people would think it was desperate or pitiful to see me spending so much time with them."

"I don't know about desperate or pitiful." Luke flashed that dimple again. "But they might think you need to be committed for a psych eval."

"No way. Anyone who spends more than five minutes with the boys sees that they're smart and talented and have so much love to give. I adore them, Luke."

"That's a relief. I'm not the best communicator, but you need to know up front that the boys and I are a package deal. I come with a lot of baggage, which is why I haven't even attempted to pursue a relationship before. I haven't felt like I deserved one and I didn't want to jeopardize the bond you share with them. But now that I've spent time with you, I don't think I could stand it if you walked out that door."

She took his face in her hands and kissed him lightly. "I love you, Luke Gregson," she said around the lump of emotion in her throat. "And I love your package deal. I'd been trying to protect myself, trying to avoid getting hurt. But it was a losing battle. I'd already surrendered my heart."

And with that admission, Carmen forced him to his back and rocked her body into place above his. Her long hair formed an intimate curtain around them as she kissed him with all the emotion she'd been holding inside.

His pulse seemed to be throbbing everywhere she touched him—against his temple, against his stomach, against the rigid hardness of his manhood. She tore at the Velcro cover of his board shorts and lifted her hips to allow him to pull her bikini bottoms off her.

She balanced on one knee to get the material past her ankle and he took advantage of her precarious position by rolling her underneath him.

He was hard and swift when he entered her, only pausing long enough to fuse his lips to hers and for her to get acclimated to his thickness. She felt him slide out of her and locked her legs around his waist, preventing him from withdrawing too much.

"I'm not going anywhere, sweetheart," he whispered in her hair, and Carmen realized he didn't just mean tonight. "And I'm not letting you run off again, either."

But Carmen no longer wanted to leave. She wanted to stay right where she was. She moaned as he sank deeper inside her. Actually, she *didn't* want to stay right here. She wanted to move with him. She wanted to move *for* him.

When his body lifted slightly, she rotated her hips and arched her spine, forcing him to lean back onto his haunches. But he took her with him, wrapping his arms around her waist as she sat up, bringing her breast to his mouth.

She moved quicker, rising higher and sinking deeper with each stroke of his tongue until he pulled his mouth away and said, "Not yet. We have to slow down or I'll…"

He didn't say what would happen, he simply hiked her up, his hands supporting her bottom as he repositioned her on the bed.

They fought for control, shifting their bodies so each one took turns being on top. His slow pace was no match for her frantic need and when she rose above him for the last time, she couldn't wait any longer.

"Now, Carmen," Luke whispered, reaching up to rub the sensitive spot directly above where their bodies met. And, like a good soldier, she followed his orders, calling out his name until every breath had left her lungs.

She tried to remain upright afterward, the conquering victor, but she was emotionally and physically spent and it was time for her to stop trying to control the situation and to just feel.

Before, making love had been sobering, but with Luke, it was intoxicating. And right now, she was drunk on pleasure.

Luke slowly stroked Carmen's naked back as she slept soundly beside him. They had made love a second time and he was hoping for a third round before it got too late in the morning.

"Carmen," he whispered, not wanting to wake her but not knowing when they'd get another opportunity to be alone. "The boys are going to be back soon."

"How soon?" Her voice sounded groggy—due to his keeping her up most of the night—and a little hoarse—due to all the cheering she'd done at the baseball field yesterday.

"Maybe an hour or so, depending on whether or not they have Honey Smacks at the free breakfast buffet. Yesterday, they stayed there eating until the cereal dispenser was empty."

"What are we going to tell them?" she asked.

"That they can have a bagel if their favorite cereal is already gone."

"Not about breakfast." She playfully pushed at his chest. "About us."

He laughed and intertwined his fingers with hers. "I'm going to tell them that you tried to go AWOL last night, but that I went rogue and retrieved you before you could cross enemy lines."

"Enemy lines? Really?"

"No?" He smiled mischievously, the way his twins often did when they wanted to charm her.

"There goes that dimple, again." But this time, she smiled back at him. "Maybe we should meet the kids at breakfast and tell them then?"

"I figure after the way you threw yourself at me in front of Elaine Marconi, we probably won't have to tell the twins anything. The whole town is going to know that we are officially a couple."

Carmen squeezed her eyes closed. "Don't remind me about that woman." When Luke laughed again, Carmen reached up her hand and used her thumb to trace around his lips.

"If you keep touching me like that, I'm going to remind you about a lot more that happened last night."

Yet, before Luke could demonstrate, he heard a steady stream of voices from the hallway outside.

"It's the boys," Carmen said, panic taking over the desire in her eyes. "I don't want them to know I spent the night here. But they'll see me if I try to go out to my room now."

Luke stacked his hands behind his head and stretched out, as if he didn't have a care in the world. "You know, my nana always said, 'Step onto the dance floor with both feet.'"

She jumped out of bed, pulling the sheet with her and wrapping it around her body. "Well, my abuela always said, '*El que no transa, no avanza.*'"

"What does that mean?"

"It means he who does not yield, does not advance."

"That actually explains a lot about you," Luke said, then dodged the pillow she threw at his head.

Rap, rap, rap, rap. Bang, bang. Tap, tap, tap, tap.

Both Carmen and Luke pivoted toward the door. "Dad, it's time for breakfast. Are you in there, Dad?"

"How am I going to get back to my room now?" she whispered.

Luke looked at the adjoining door between their rooms and his brain clicked on something he would have done back when he was nine. He pointed. "Just go through there."

"Luke, don't be absurd. Hotels usually have locks on both sides of the doors."

"Have you met my children?" he asked. "They've never met a lock that could keep them out of trouble."

She gave him a doubtful look before pushing on the door. When it sprang open, the empty toilet paper roll that the twins must have wedged into the latch fell to the ground.

Just as the secret knock sounded on Carmen's hotel door.

Rap, rap, rap, rap. Bang, bang. Tap, tap, tap, tap.

"Hey, Officer Carmen. If our dad's still in there with you, tell him they're out of Honey Smacks so we're going to walk to the doughnut store down the street with Choogie."

She looked back at Luke, and he lifted his arms and shrugged his shoulders. "What can I say? They'll always be one step ahead of us." He pulled on his shorts and tossed her the discarded cotton dress she'd been wearing over her bathing suit last night. "Besides, Officer Carmen, I'm done with hiding and pretending I can control myself around you. No more guilt, no more regrets, right?"

She nodded. "The Marine Corps taught me to never leave a man behind. But since you're the higher ranking officer, I'll let you do the explaining."

She slipped on her dress, then followed Luke through the adjoining room.

"Okay, you monkeys," he said when he opened her hotel room door. "You're going to wake the entire floor."

The twins rushed inside. "Hey, are you guys coming down for breakfast or what?" Aiden asked.

"And if you're in Officer Carmen's room already, does this mean she's your girlfriend now?" Caden wanted to know.

Luke covered his mouth to smother the chuckling sound he'd just made. Then he raised an eyebrow at Carmen, but she clearly wasn't going to get him out of this mess. Maybe he should've let her sneak back into her room when they'd had the chance.

"Well, I haven't quite asked Carmen if she was willing to become my girlfriend, yet," he said.

"You want us to help you ask her?" Aiden was

rocking on the balls of his feet, his bright smile turned her way.

"I think she'll say yes, Dad." Caden's grin was equally bright.

Carmen was smiling along with them. "And why would you think that?" she asked.

"Because then you'd get to see us all the time and not just on Tuesdays or when we get into trouble."

"Hmmm…" She pretended to ponder the decision. "I don't suppose I could resist an offer like that."

"So then I guess my work here is done," Luke said, wrapping an arm around her and pulling her in close. "Let's go get some breakfast with my new girlfriend."

The twins each grabbed one of her hands and pulled her toward the door.

"Wait," Carmen squeaked. "I need to get ready first."

"Ready for what? You're already dressed." Aiden continued to tug on her arm. "Grammie and Pop Pop are waiting for us. Besides, we need to get downstairs and tell Choogie our plan worked."

"Why don't you boys go down now," Luke suggested. "We'll get ready and meet everyone there in a few minutes."

The boys gave one last whoop, high-fived each other and ran off toward the elevators.

"What plan do you think they were talking about?" she asked when they were alone in the room again.

"I have absolutely no idea," he admitted. "But I have a feeling Choogie isn't the only one they're going to tell the good news to."

"That reminds me. We should probably talk to the person who runs the announcement booth at the baseball field and advise them not to let any nine-year-old twins near the loudspeaker today."

Luke laughed. "You sound like you know what you're getting into with us."

"I certainly like challenging jobs."

"You made them very happy, you know." Luke traced a finger under the shoulder strap of her dress. "And now it would make me very happy to help you take this thing off and get ready."

When Luke's lips touched her cheek, Carmen said, "I feel like the happiest one of all."

Epilogue

Carmen threw away a handful of napkins after cleaning up the spilled punch on the floor next to Caden, who wasn't technically her date for tonight's Mother-Son Dancing Safari. Walking back to where a group of third-grade boys were finishing off the last batch of cookies donated by the Sugar Falls Cookie Company, she tried not to scratch at the homemade pinecone corsage on her wrist.

The DJ had announced the last song, and while Aiden danced with his aunt Kylie, several of the teachers and parents were already cleaning up, trying to turn the decorated room back into the school cafeteria.

She felt Luke's hands around her waist before she heard his voice. "Remember the last time we were in this room together?" he asked.

"I remember being a little higher off the ground,"

she said, placing her hands on his and leaning her head back into his shoulder.

He nodded his head toward the safari-themed wall hanging being taken down. "Yeah, and our monkeys were the only wildlife in here at the time."

Our monkeys. Carmen felt a rush of warm, tingly happiness and looked at Caden and Aiden, who'd finished dancing and joined his brother and their friends.

"My feet are killing me," Kylie Gregson said as she teetered in their direction wearing a five-inch pair of stilettos. "I haven't danced this much since the Boise State Spirit Squad Reunion."

Carmen had to admit the former cheerleader had a great sense of style and had outlasted all the other moms on the dance floor.

"Drew's waiting in the car," Luke told his sister-in-law.

"We could have driven ourselves," Carmen said, used to being independent and talking care of herself.

"No way." Luke smiled at her, then looked up to see the twins walking up. "The boys wanted this to be a full-service event."

"We tried to order a limo," Caden said. "But Dad said he had more expensive things to buy."

She turned to Luke, but not before the corner of her eye caught Aiden shooting an elbow to his brother's ribs.

"Hey, look," Luke said, reaching behind him for a chocolate pudding cup that Carmen could have sworn hadn't been on that table just a minute ago. "Remember the last time we shared one of these?"

Carmen raised her eyebrow. What was up with Luke's little trip down memory lane? "Yep. I thought Scooter and Jonesy had finished off the last of them."

"Apparently not all of them." Luke held the plastic container under her nose. "Here. You should have the last one."

"Oh, no thanks." Carmen wrinkled her nose. "I already had a ton of cookies from Maxine's bakery, and the only drink they offered tonight was that neon-red punch. I'm all sugared out."

"Just open the pudding cup, Carmen." She noticed the perspiration on Luke's brow and wondered if he was getting impatient because the boys were giggling and jumping around like a couple of caged hyenas.

"Come on, boys," Kylie said, waving her wrist with the matching pinecone corsage in the air. "Let's go wait out in the car with Uncle Drew."

"No way. We want to stay for this. Me and Caden worked way too hard on this project for the past few months. We're not gonna miss out on the bestest part of the night."

Carmen looked at the matching set of nine-year-old grins and could only imagine what kind of project they'd organized this time. But when she turned back to their dad, her breath caught in her chest and she had to blink several times to clear her eyes.

Luke was down on one knee, the foil wrapper of his pudding cup peeled back to reveal a diamond solitaire halfway buried in chocolate. "I love you, Maria Carmen Delgado."

"*We* love you," Caden corrected his father.

Luke nodded. "We love you, Maria Carmen Delgado. Will you marry me?"

"Marry *us*, Dad." Aiden got down next to his father. "You were supposed to ask if she'd marry *us*."

Caden joined the other two Gregsons on their knees

and Carmen, who always knew how to handle men, suddenly didn't know how she would handle being this happy.

"Of course, I will marry all of you!"

The boys jumped up, shouting and high-fiving, leaving their father still kneeling and holding the ring, which was now sinking down lower into the pudding. Carmen knelt beside him, and he dug the diamond out, then licked it off before putting it on her finger.

She laughed and kissed him, his mouth tasting like chocolate.

"I love you, too," she said, but Luke's attention was already on his celebrating sons, a look of suspicion on his face.

"Wait a minute. You guys said you'd worked too hard on this project for the past few months. But we only went to the jewelry store in Boise last weekend."

Kylie, who'd just snapped a picture of the pudding proposal, tossed her cell phone into her beaded designer clutch.

"I better go check on Drew," she said, leaving in an obvious hurry. His sister-in-law's abrupt departure must've put Luke on even higher alert, because he hadn't looked away from the smiling twins long enough to say goodbye.

"You boys have something you want to explain?" he asked when his sons both took a sudden interest in the design of the ceiling.

Aiden nudged Caden, who shot a frown at his brother before finally speaking. "We heard you tell the other dads at poker night that you wanted Officer Carmen to like you. And since we knew she liked us, we decided to get her to like you, too."

"But that was months ago." Luke, still looking perplexed, remained on his knees. "How did you come up with...?"

Carmen saw the realization hit his face seconds after it hit hers. "Did you guys plan this all on your own?"

"Mostly. But we had to get a whole bunch of help from everyone to make it work."

Like a movie reel playing in her mind, Carmen flashed back to the tipped canoe, the last-minute trip for party supplies, the hotel room next to theirs suddenly becoming available. All along, she'd been outsmarted and outplayed by a couple of nine-year-old twins. Then she started laughing, realizing that it probably wouldn't be the last time.

"You two little matchmakers are lucky this harebrained scheme of yours worked out and that Carmen and I ended up falling in love." Luke pulled both of his sons in for a tight hug.

The boys giggled again and Caden said, "Uncle Kane told us there was no such thing as luck."

"Oh, really," Luke said, standing and pulling Carmen into his arms. "You tell Uncle Kane that he just needs the right good luck charm."

* * * * *

Look for Kane Chatterson's story,
the next installment in Christy Jeffries's
new miniseries
SUGAR FALLS, IDAHO,
coming soon to Harlequin Special Edition!
And don't miss the previous books in this miniseries:

A MARINE FOR HIS MOM
WAKING UP WED
and
FROM DARE TO DUE DATE.

Available wherever Harlequin books
and ebooks are sold!

*Officer Wyn Bailey has found herself
wanting more from her boss—and older
brother's best friend—for a while now.
Will sexy police chief Cade Emmett let
his guard down long enough to embrace
the love he secretly craves?*

Read on for a sneak peek at the newest book in
New York Times *bestselling author
RaeAnne Thayne's* HAVEN POINT *series,*
RIVERBEND ROAD,
available July 2016 from HQN Books.

CHAPTER ONE

"THIS WAS YOUR dire emergency? Seriously?"

Officer Wynona Bailey leaned against her Haven Point Police Department squad car, not sure whether to laugh or pull out her hair. "That frantic phone call made it sound like you were at death's door!" she exclaimed to her great-aunt Jenny. "You mean to tell me I drove here with full lights and sirens, afraid I would stumble over you bleeding on the ground, only to find you in a standoff with a baby moose?"

The gangly-looking creature had planted himself in the middle of the driveway while he browsed from the shrubbery that bordered it. He paused in his chewing to watch the two of them out of long-lashed dark eyes.

He was actually really cute, with big ears and a curious face. She thought about pulling out her phone to take a picture that her sister could hang on the local wildlife bulletin board in her classroom but decided Jenny probably wouldn't appreciate it.

"It's not the calf I'm worried about," her great-aunt said. "It's his mama over there."

She followed her aunt's gaze and saw a female moose on the other side of the willow shrubs, watching them with much more caution than her baby was showing.

While the creature might look docile on the outside,

Wyn knew from experience a thousand-pound cow could move at thirty-five miles an hour and wouldn't hesitate to take on anything she perceived as a threat to her offspring.

"I need to get into my garage, that's all," Jenny practically wailed. "If Baby Bullwinkle there would just move two feet onto the lawn, I could squeeze around him, but he won't budge for anything."

She had to ask the logical question. "Did you try honking your horn?"

Aunt Jenny glared at her, looking as fierce and stern as she used to when Wynona was late turning in an assignment in her aunt's high school history class.

"Of course I tried honking my horn! And hollering at the stupid thing and even driving right up to him, as close as I could get, which only made the mama come over to investigate. I had to back up again."

Wyn's blood ran cold, imagining the scene. That big cow could easily charge the sporty little convertible her diminutive great-aunt had bought herself on her seventy-fifth birthday.

What would make them move along? Wynona sighed, not quite sure what trick might disperse a couple of stubborn moose. Sure, she was trained in Krav Maga martial arts, but somehow none of those lessons seemed to apply in this situation.

The pair hadn't budged when she pulled up with her lights and sirens blaring in answer to her aunt's desperate phone call. Even if she could get them to move, scaring them out of Aunt Jenny's driveway would probably only migrate the problem to the neighbor's yard.

She was going to have to call in backup from the state wildlife division.

"Oh, no!" her aunt suddenly wailed. "He's starting on the honeysuckle! He's going to ruin it. Stop! Move it. Go on now." Jenny started to climb out of her car again, raising and lowering her arms like a football referee calling a touchdown.

"Aunt Jenny, get back inside your vehicle!" Wyn exclaimed.

"But the honeysuckle! Your dad planted that for me the summer before he…well, you know."

Wyn's heart gave a sharp little spasm. Yes. She *did* know. She pictured the sturdy, robust man who had once watched over his aunt, along with everybody else in town. He wouldn't have hesitated for a second here, would have known exactly how to handle the situation.

Wynnie, anytime you're up against something bigger than you, just stare 'em down. More often than not, that will do the trick.

Some days, she almost felt like he was riding shotgun next to her.

"Stay in your car, Jenny," she said again. "Just wait there while I call Idaho Fish and Game to handle things. They probably need to move them to higher ground."

"I don't have time to wait for some yahoo to load up his tranq gun and hitch up his horse trailer, then drive over from Shelter Springs! Besides that honeysuckle, which is priceless to me, I have seventy-eight dollars' worth of groceries in the trunk of my car that will be ruined if I can't get into the house. That includes four pints of Ben & Jerry's Cherry Garcia that's going to be melted red goo if I don't get it in the freezer fast—and that stuff is not exactly cheap, you know."

Her great-aunt looked at her with every expectation that she would fix the problem and Wyn sighed again. Small-town police work was mostly about problem solving—and when she happened to have been born and raised in that small town, too many people treated her like their own private security force.

"I get it. But I'm calling Fish and Game."

"You've got a piece. Can't you just fire it into the air or something?"

Yeah, unfortunately, her great-aunt—like everybody else in town—watched far too many cop dramas on TV and thought that was how things were done.

"Give me two minutes to call Fish and Game, then I'll see if I can get him to move aside enough that you can pull into your driveway. Wait in your car," she ordered for the fourth time as she kept an eye on Mama Moose. "Do not, I repeat, do *not* get out again. Promise?"

Aunt Jenny slumped back into her seat, clearly disappointed that she wasn't going to have front row seats to some kind of moose-cop shoot-out. "I suppose."

To Wyn's relief, local game warden Moose Porter—who, as far as she knew, was no relation to the current troublemakers—picked up on the first ring. She explained the situation to him and gave him the address.

"You're in luck. We just got back from relocating a female brown bear and her cub away from that campground on Dry Creek Road. I've still got the trailer hitched up."

"Thanks. I owe you."

"How about that dinner we've been talking about?" he asked.

She had not been talking about dinner. Moose had been pretty relentless in asking her out for months and she always managed to deflect. It wasn't that she didn't like the guy. He was nice and funny and good-looking in a burly, outdoorsy, flannel-shirt-and-gun-rack sort of way, but she didn't feel so much as an ember around him. Not like, well, someone else she preferred not to think about.

Maybe she would stop thinking about that *someone else* if she ever bothered to go on a date. "Sure," she said on impulse. "I'm pretty busy until after Lake Haven Days, but let's plan something in a couple of weeks. Meantime, how soon can you be here?"

"Great! I'll definitely call you. And I've got an ETA of about seven minutes now."

The obvious delight left her squirming and wishing she had deflected his invitation again.

Fish or cut line, her father would have said.

"Make it five, if you can. My great-aunt's favorite honeysuckle bush is in peril here."

"On it."

She ended the phone call just as Jenny groaned, "Oh. Not the butterfly bush, too! Shoo. Go on, move!"

While she was on the phone, the cow had moved around the shrubs nearer her calf and was nibbling on the large showy blossoms on the other side of the driveway.

Wyn thought about waiting for the game warden to handle the situation, but Jenny was counting on her. She couldn't let a couple of moose get the better of her. Wondering idly if a Kevlar vest would protect her in the event she was charged, she climbed out of her patrol vehicle and edged around to the front bumper. "Come on. Move along. That's it."

She opted to move toward the calf, figuring the cow would follow her baby. Mindful to keep the vehicle between her and the bigger animal, she waved her arms like she was directing traffic in a big-city intersection. "Go. Get out of here."

Something in her firm tone or maybe her rapid-fire movements finally must have convinced the calf she wasn't messing around this time. He paused for just a second, then lurched through a break in the shrubs to the other side, leaving just enough room for Great-Aunt Jenny to squeeze past and head for her garage to unload her groceries.

"Thank you, Wynnie. You're the best," her aunt called. "Come by one of these Sundays for dinner. I'll make my fried chicken and biscuits and my Better-Than-Sex cake."

Her mouth watered and her stomach rumbled, reminding her quite forcefully that she hadn't eaten anything since her shift started that morning.

Her great-aunt's Sunday dinners were pure decadence. Wyn could almost feel her arteries clog in anticipation.

"I'll check my schedule."

"Thanks again."

Jenny drove her flashy little convertible into the garage and quickly closed the door behind her.

Of all things, the sudden action of the door seemed to startle the big cow moose where all other efforts—including a honking horn and Wyn's yelling and arm-peddling—had failed. The moose shied away from the activity, heading in Wyn's direction.

Crap.

Heart pounding, she managed to jump into her vehicle and yank the door closed behind her seconds before the moose charged past her toward the calf.

The two big animals picked their way across the lawn and settled in to nibble Jenny's pretty red-twig dogwoods.

Crisis managed—or at least her part in it—she turned around and drove back to the street just as a pickup pulling a trailer with the Idaho Fish and Game logo came into view over the hill.

She pushed the button to roll down her window and Moose did the same. Beside him sat a game warden she didn't know. Moose beamed at her and she squirmed, wishing she had shut him down again instead of giving him unrealistic expectations.

"It's a cow and her calf," she said, forcing her tone into a brisk, businesslike one and addressing both men in the vehicle. "They're now on the south side of the house."

"Thanks for running recon for us," Moose said.

"Yeah. Pretty sure we managed to save the Ben & Jerry's, so I guess my work here is done."

The warden grinned at her and she waved and pulled onto the road, leaving her window down for the sweet-smelling June breezes to float in.

She couldn't really blame a couple of moose for wandering into town for a bit of lunch. This was a beautiful time around Lake Haven, when the wildflowers were starting to bloom and the grasses were long and lush.

She loved Haven Point with all her heart, but she found it pretty sad that the near-moose encounter was the most exciting thing that had happened to her on the job in days.

Her cell phone rang just as she turned from Clover Hill Road to Lakeside Drive. She knew by the ringtone just who was on the other end and her breathing hitched a little, like always. Those stone-cold embers she had been wondering about when it came to Moose Porter suddenly flared to thick, crackling life.

Yeah. She knew at least one reason why she didn't go out much.

She pushed the phone button on her vehicle's hands-free unit. "Hey, Chief."

"Hear you had a little excitement this afternoon and almost tangled with a couple of moose."

She heard the amusement in the voice of her boss—and friend—and tried not to picture Cade Emmett stretched out behind his desk, big and rangy and gorgeous, with that surprisingly sweet smile that broke hearts all over Lake Haven County.

"News travels."

"Your great-aunt Jenny just called to inform me you risked your life to save her Cherry Garcia and to tell me all about how you deserve a special commendation."

"If she really thought that, why didn't she at least give me a pint for my trouble?" she grumbled.

The police chief laughed, that rich, full laugh that made her fingers and toes tingle like she'd just run full tilt down Clover Hill Road with her arms outspread.

Curse the man.

"You'll have to take that up with her next time you see her. Meantime, we just got a call about possible trespassers at that old wreck of a barn on Darwin Twitchell's horse property on Conifer Drive, just before the turnoff for Riverbend. Would you mind checking it out before you head back for the shift change?"

"Who called it in?"

"Darwin. Apparently somebody tripped an alarm he set up after he got hit by our friendly local graffiti artist a few weeks back."

Leave it to the ornery old buzzard to set a trap for unsuspecting trespassers. Knowing Darwin and his contrariness, he probably installed infrared sweepers and body heat sensors, even though the ramshackle barn held absolutely nothing of value.

"The way my luck is going today, it's probably a relative to the two moose I just made friends with."

"It could be a skunk, for all I know. But Darwin made me swear I'd send an officer to check it out. Since the graffiti case is yours, I figured you'd want first dibs, just in case you have the chance to catch them red-handed. Literally."

"Gosh, thanks."

He chuckled again and the warmth of it seemed to ease through the car even through the hollow, tinny Bluetooth speakers.

"Keep me posted."

"Ten-four."

She turned her vehicle around and headed in the general direction of her own little stone house on Riverbend Road that used to belong to her grandparents.

The Redemption mountain range towered across the lake, huge and imposing. The snow that would linger in the moraines and ridges above the timberline for at least another month gleamed in the afternoon sunlight, and the lake was that pure, vivid turquoise usually seen only in shallow Caribbean waters.

Her job as one of six full-time officers in the Haven Point Police Department might not always be overflowing with excitement, but she couldn't deny that her workplace surroundings were pretty gorgeous.

She spotted the first tendrils of black smoke above the treetops as she turned onto the rutted lane that wound its way through pale aspen trunks and thick pines and spruce.

Probably just a nearby farmer burning some weeds along a ditch line, she told herself, or trying to get rid of the bushy-topped invasive phragmites reeds that could encroach into any marshy areas and choke out all the native species. But something about the black curl of smoke hinted at a situation beyond a controlled burn.

Her stomach fluttered with nerves. She hated fire calls even more than the dreaded DD—domestic disturbance. At least in a domestic situation, there was some chance she could defuse the conflict. Fire was avaricious and relentless, smoke and flame and terror. She had learned that lesson on one of her first calls as a green-as-grass rookie police officer in Boise, when she was the first one on scene to a deadly house fire on a cold January morning that had killed three children in their sleep.

Wyn rounded the last bend in the road and saw, just as feared, the smoke wasn't coming from a ditch line or a controlled burn of a patch of invading plants. Instead, it twisted sinuously into the sky from the ramshackle barn on Darwin Twitchell's property.

She scanned the area for kids and couldn't see any. What she did see made her blood run cold—two small boys' bikes resting on their sides outside the barn.

Where there were bikes, there were usually boys to ride them.

She parked her vehicle and shoved open her door. "Hello? Anybody here?" she called.

She strained her ears but could hear nothing above the crackle of flames. Heat and flames poured off the building.

She pressed the button on the radio at her shoulder to call dispatch. "I've got a structure fire, an old barn on Darwin Twitchell's property on Conifer Drive, just before Riverbend Road. The upper part seems to be fully engulfed and there's a possibility of civilians inside, juveniles. I've got bikes here but no kids in sight. I'm still looking."

While she raced around the building, she heard the call go out to the volunteer fire department and Chief Gallegos respond that his crews were six minutes out.

"Anybody here?" she called again.

Just faintly, she thought she heard a high cry in response, but her radio crackled with static at that instant and she couldn't be sure. A second later, she heard Cade's voice.

"Bailey, this is Chief Emmett. What's the status of the kids? Over."

She hurried back to her vehicle and popped the trunk. "I can't see them," she answered tersely, digging for a couple of water bottles and an extra T-shirt she kept back there. "I'm going in."

"Negative!" Cade's urgency fairly crackled through

the radio. "The first fire crew's ETA is now four minutes. Stand down."

She turned back to the fire and was almost positive the flames seemed to be crackling louder, the smoke billowing higher into the sky. She couldn't stand the thought of children being caught inside that hellish scene. She couldn't. She pushed away the memory of those tiny charred bodies.

Maybe whoever had tripped Darwin's alarms— maybe the same kids who likely set the fire—had run off into the surrounding trees. She hoped so, she really did, but her gut told her otherwise.

In four minutes, they could be burned to a crisp, just like those sweet little kids in Boise. She had to take a look.

It's what her father would have done.

You know what John Wayne would say, John Bailey's voice seemed to echo in her head. *Courage is being scared to death but saddling up, anyway.*

Yeah, Dad. I know.

Her hands were sweaty with fear, but she pushed past it and focused on the situation at hand. "I'm going in," she repeated.

"Stand down, Officer Bailey. That is a direct order."

Cade ran a fairly casual—though efficient—police department and rarely pushed rank, but right now he sounded hard, dangerous.

She paused for only a second, her attention caught by sunlight glinting off one of the bikes.

"Wynona, do you copy?" Cade demanded.

She couldn't do it. She couldn't stand out here and wait for the fire department. Time was of the essence, she knew it in her bones. After five years as a police officer, she had learned to rely on her instincts and she couldn't ignore them now.

She was just going to have to disregard his order and deal with his fury later.

"I can't hear you," she lied. "Sorry. You're crackling out."

She squelched her radio to keep him out of her ears, ripped the T-shirt and doused it with her water bottle, then held it to her mouth and pushed inside.

The shift from sunlight to smoke and darkness inside the barn was disorienting. As she had seen from outside, the flames seemed to be limited for now to the upper hayloft of the barn, but the air was thick and acrid.

"Hello?" she called out. "Anybody here?"

"Yes! Help!"

"Please help!"

Two distinct, high, terrified voices came from the far end of the barn.

"Okay. Okay," she called back, her heart pounding fiercely. "Keep talking so I can follow your voice."

There was a momentary pause. "What should we say?"

"Sing a song. How about 'Jingle Bells'? Here. I'll start."

She started the words off and then stopped when she heard two young voices singing the words between sobs. She whispered a quick prayer for help and courage, then rapidly picked her way over rubble and debris as she followed the song to its source, which turned out to be two white-faced, terrified boys she knew.

Caleb and Lucas Keegan were crouched together

just below a ladder up to the loft, where the flames sizzled and popped overhead.

Caleb, the older of the two, was stretched out on the ground, his leg bent at an unnatural angle.

"Hey, Caleb. Hey, Luke."

They both sobbed when they spotted her. "Officer Bailey. We didn't mean to start the fire! We didn't mean to!" Luke, the younger one, was close to hysteria, but she didn't have time to calm him.

"We can worry about that later. Right now, we need to get out of here."

"We tried, but Caleb broked his leg! He fell and he can't walk. I was trying to pull him out, but I'm not strong enough."

"I told him to go without me," the older boy, no more than ten, said through tears. "I screamed and screamed at him, but he wouldn't go."

"We're all getting out of here." She ripped the wet cloth in half and handed a section to each boy.

Yeah, she knew the whole adage—taught by the airline industry, anyway—about taking care of yourself before turning your attention to helping others, but this case was worth an exception.

"Caleb, I'm going to pick you up. It's going to hurt, especially if I bump that broken leg of yours, but I don't have time to give you first aid."

"It doesn't matter. I don't care. Do what you have to do. We have to get Luke out of here!"

Her eyes burned from the smoke and her throat felt tight and achy. If she had time to spare, she would have wept at the boy's quiet courage. "I'm sorry," she whispered. She scooped him up into a fireman's carry, finally appreciating the efficiency of the hold. He probably weighed close to eighty pounds, but adrenaline gave her strength.

Over the crackles and crashes overhead, she heard him swallow a scream as his ankle bumped against her.

"Luke, grab hold of my belt buckle, right there in the back. That's it. Do not let go, no matter what. You hear me?"

"Yes," the boy whispered.

"I can't carry you both. I wish I could. You ready?"

"I'm scared," Luke whimpered through the wet T-shirt wrapped around his mouth.

So am I, kiddo. She forced a confident smile she was far from feeling. "Stay close to me. We're tough. We can do this."

The pep talk was meant for herself, more than the boys. Flames had finally begun crawling down the side of the barn and it didn't take long for the fire to slither its way through the old hay and debris scattered through the place.

She did *not* want to run through those flames, but her dad's voice seemed to ring again in her ears.

You never know how strong you are until being strong is the only choice you've got.

Okay, okay. She got it, already.

She ran toward the door, keeping Caleb on her shoulder with one hand while she wrapped her other around Luke's neck.

They were just feet from the door when the younger boy stumbled and went down. She could hear the flames growling louder and knew the dry, rotten barn wood was going to combust any second.

With no time to spare, she half lifted him with her

other arm and dragged them all through the door and into the sunshine while the fire licked and growled at their heels.

* * * * *

Don't miss RIVERBEND ROAD by
New York Times *bestselling author*
RaeAnne Thayne,
available July 2016 wherever HQN books
and ebooks are sold.
www.Harlequin.com

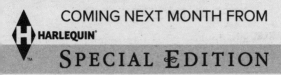

COMING NEXT MONTH FROM

HARLEQUIN®

SPECIAL EDITION

Available July 19, 2016

#2491 HER MAVERICK M.D.
Montana Mavericks: The Baby Bonanza • by Teresa Southwick
Nurse Dawn Laramie refuses to fall for a doctor she works with and put her job at risk...again! But Jonathon Clifton won't let her cold shoulder get to him. When these two finally bury the hatchet and become friends, will they be able to resist the wild attraction between them?

#2492 AN UNLIKELY DADDY
Conard County: The Next Generation • by Rachel Lee
Pregnant widow Marisa Hayes is still grieving her husband's death when his best friend, Ryker Tremaine, arrives on her doorstep. He promised to watch out for Marisa in case anything happened to Johnny, but the more time he spends with her, the more he longs to help her through her grief to a new life—and love—with him.

#2493 HIS BADGE, HER BABY...THEIR FAMILY?
Men of the West • by Stella Bagwell
Geena and Vince Parcell were married once before, until the stress of Vince's job as a police detective took its toll. Six years later, when Geena shows up in Carson City pregnant and missing her memories, they have a second chance at becoming the family they always wanted.

#2494 A DOG AND A DIAMOND
The McKinnels of Jewell Rock • by Rachael Johns
The closest thing Chelsea Porter has to a family is her beloved dog. When she attends the McKinnel family Thanksgiving with Callum McKinnel, she finds the love and warmth she's always craved. Can they work through their fears from the past to make a future together?

#2495 ALWAYS THE BEST MAN
Crimson, Colorado • by Michelle Major
After a nasty divorce, Emily Whittaker is back in Crimson with her son. Jase Crenshaw thought he was over his high school crush on Emily, but when they team up as best man and maid of honor for her brother's wedding, Jase thinks he's finally found his chance to win the girl of his dreams...

#2496 THE DOCTOR'S RUNAWAY FIANCÉE
Rx for Love • by Cindy Kirk
When Sylvie Thorne broke their engagement, Dr. Andrew O'Shea realized he didn't know the woman he loved at all. So when he finds out she's in Wyoming, he decides to get some answers. Sylvie still thinks she made the right decision, but when Andrew moves in to get closure, she's not sure she'll be able to resist the man he becomes away from his high-society family.

**YOU CAN FIND MORE INFORMATION ON UPCOMING HARLEQUIN® TITLES,
FREE EXCERPTS AND MORE AT WWW.HARLEQUIN.COM.**

HSECNM0716

"Am I awful?"

"Awful? What in the world would make you think that?"

"Because…because…" She put her face in her hands.

At once Ryker squatted beside her, worried, touching her arm. "Marisa? What's wrong?"

"Nothing. It's just… I shouldn't be having these feelings."

"What feelings?" Suicidal thoughts? Urges to kill someone? Fear? The whole palette of emotions lay there waiting for her to choose one.

She kept her face covered. "I have dreams about you."

His entire body leaped. He had dreams about her, too, and not only when he was sleeping. "And?"

"I want you. Is that wrong? I mean…it hasn't been that long…"

Her words deprived him of breath. He could have lifted her right then and carried her to her bed. He'd have done so joyfully. But caution and maybe even some wisdom held him back.

"I want you, too," he said huskily.

She dropped her hands, her wondering eyes meeting his almost shyly. "Really? Looking like this?"

"You're beautiful looking just like that. But…"

"But?" She seized on the word, some of the wonder leaving her face.

"I don't want you to regret it. So how about we spend more time talking to each other? Give yourself some time to be sure. Hell, it probably wouldn't be safe anyway."

"My doc says it would."

She'd asked her doctor? A thousand explosions went off in his head, leaving him almost blind. He cleared his throat. "Uh…I could take you right now. I want to. So, please, don't be embarrassed. I don't think you're awful. But…please… get to know me a bit better. I want to know you better. I want you to be sure."

"I feel guilty," she admitted. "It's been driving me nuts. Am I betraying Johnny?"

"I don't believe he'd think so. But that's a question only you can answer, and you need to do that for yourself. Then there's me."

"You?" She studied him.

"I don't exactly feel right about this. After what you've already been through, I shouldn't have to explain that. I'm just like John, Marisa. Why in the world would you want to risk that again?"

She nodded slowly, looking down at where her fingertips pressed into the wooden table. "I don't know," she finally said quietly.

Don't miss
AN UNLIKELY DADDY
by New York Times *bestselling author Rachel Lee,*
available August 2016 wherever
Harlequin® Special Edition books and ebooks are sold.

www.Harlequin.com

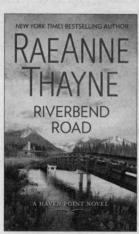

THE WORLD IS BETTER WITH

Romance

Harlequin has everything from contemporary, passionate and heartwarming to suspenseful and inspirational stories.

Whatever your mood, we have a romance just for you!

Connect with us to find your next great read, special offers and more.

f /HarlequinBooks

@HarlequinBooks

www.HarlequinBlog.com

www.Harlequin.com/Newsletters

◆ HARLEQUIN®

A *Romance* FOR EVERY MOOD™

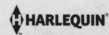

www.Harlequin.com